Redhall Riders

Amanda Wills

ISBN: 1530227569
ISBN-13: 978-1530227563

To my wonderful readers. You make this writing business, pencils and what-not, so much fun.

CHAPTER 1

Poppy McKeever knew that the haunting cry of the curlew would forever remind her of the accident. *Coor-lee, coor-lee, coor-lee* called the bird into the vast Dartmoor sky as Cloud thundered across the moor towards the isolated farm they had passed an hour earlier. Poppy crouched low over the saddle, urging her pony faster. Cloud, his ears flat and his nostrils flared, responded by lengthening his stride until they were galloping flat out. Poppy wound her hands through his silver mane and chanced a look back, but the others were already tiny specks on the horizon. An old stone wall loomed ahead and she eased Cloud back into a canter. Seeing a stride she squeezed her calves and he soared over the wall with a foot to spare, landing nimbly on the spongey grass on the far side. They turned right, following the steam as it dipped and curved towards the farm, Poppy's heart crashing in time with Cloud's pounding hooves.

Coor-lee, coor-lee, coor-lee cried the curlew from the marshland between the stream and a belt of emerald green conifers. A dark stain of sweat was seeping across Cloud's grey flanks and Poppy could feel him beginning to tire.

"Not far now," she whispered, running a hand across his neck. He flicked an ear back at the sound of her voice. "Look, I can see the farm."

With every stride the farmhouse grew bigger. Poppy remembered the rosy-cheeked woman in a red and white checked shirt who'd been picking runner beans as they'd ridden past earlier. Balancing a trug on her hip she'd called a cheery greeting and they'd waved back. Poppy hoped with all her heart that she was still at home.

They clattered up a stony track to the farmyard. Poppy slithered to the ground and looped her pony's reins over a fence post. Bella would be horrified but there was no time to waste. Cloud watched her, his ears pricked, as she ran into the farmyard, scattering a handful of chickens pecking about in the dirt. Their indignant squawking woke an elderly collie curled up on a rug by the back door. He raised his head and gave a low woof before settling back to sleep.

"Please be in," Poppy muttered, tugging at the brass door knocker. She almost wept with relief when the door swung open and the woman in the checked shirt stepped out, brushing flour from her hands.

"There's been an accident. I need to use your

phone," Poppy croaked, her mouth dry.

The woman glanced briefly at Cloud standing patiently by the fence and ushered Poppy into a shabby hallway that smelt of freshly-baked scones.

"Whatever's happened? Are you hurt?"

"Not me. One of the other riders. Her pony fell." Poppy pictured Niamh lying motionless on the ground and Merry standing next to her, the bay mare's hind leg hanging uselessly from her hock. She felt the prickle of tears. "There was no phone signal. I need to call an ambulance."

The woman handed her a phone and a tissue and watched as Poppy dialled 999. As she waited for the call to connect Poppy looked wildly around. "I don't know where we are!"

"Tell them to head for Pegworthy Farm and we can take them from here. I'll write down the postcode."

Poppy took the scrap of paper and gave the woman a grateful smile. "Thank-you."

"That's alright." She laid a hand on Poppy's arm, leaving a faint floury imprint. "Don't worry. I expect they'll send the air ambulance. Everything will be OK."

Poppy nodded. But inside her heart she knew the woman was wrong. Everything was not going to be OK.

The day had started so well. When Poppy's battered Mickey Mouse alarm clock pulled her out of a deep slumber with a persistent ringing that had bordered on impolite, she groaned, pulled the duvet over her head and almost went back to sleep. Until she remembered with a delicious jolt that it was the first day of the summer holidays. No school, no homework, no interminable talk of coursework and options for a whole six glorious weeks. And as if that wasn't exciting enough, the day she and Scarlett had been looking forward to for weeks had finally arrived.

Poppy jumped out of bed and crossed her room in a couple of strides, picking up a pair of jodhpurs from the end of her bed on the way. She flung open her bedroom window and whistled. Cloud looked up from where he was grazing in the paddock and whinnied. Chester gave an echoing heehaw. Poppy narrowed her eyes and scrutinised her pony. The Connemara had a grass stain on his dappled grey rump, a patch of mud running down his shoulder and a tangled mane. She glanced at the alarm clock. Seven o'clock. Two hours before Scarlett's dad Bill was due to arrive with the trailer to take Cloud and Scarlett's Dartmoor pony Blaze to Redhall Manor Equestrian Centre. Two hours to transform the muddy vision in front of her into a beautifully turned out pony. She knew she was lucky to be invited to Redhall for the week. The least she could do was to meet the exacting standards of Bella Thompson, Redhall's owner.

A bucket of warm water in one hand and a carrot in the other, Poppy headed out of the back door. Wisps of mist that had settled in dips and hollows the night before were already evaporating under the

4

strong midsummer sun. Cloud and Chester stood at the gate flicking flies away with their tails. Poppy measured out their breakfasts and let them into the small area of crumbling concrete in front of the stables and barn that she ambitiously called the yard. While they ate she squirted horse shampoo into the bucket and set to work on Cloud, using a sponge to rub the shampoo into his coat and her fingers to work suds into his mane and tail. She gently hosed him down and used a sweat scraper to squeeze out the excess water. Chester nudged her, as if to remind her it was his turn. Poppy kissed his nose.

"I'm sorry, Chester. You're staying at home with Caroline and Dad."

At five past nine Bill's Land Rover bounced up the Riverdale drive, the trailer swaying gently behind it. Scarlett leapt out and slammed the door.

"Poppy! We're here!"

"I heard you," grinned Poppy, emerging from the tack room with Cloud's saddle on one arm and his grooming kit in the other.

"I'll take that. You load Cloud. I've done a hay net for him." Scarlett opened the door of the Land Rover, propped the saddle alongside her own and squeezed the grooming kit into a space between a sack of sheep pellets and a metal feeding trough. "I'll get your bridle. Where's your bag?"

"Here," said Caroline, appearing from the house with Poppy's battered holdall. "The place is going to feel a bit empty with you off for the week and Charlie at Cub camp."

"Least Dad's at home," said Poppy.

Caroline nodded. "I've got a list of jobs for him, starting with clearing the guttering. He's going to wish he was at work."

Cloud safely loaded, they said goodbye and Bill nosed the Land Rover back down the drive. Soon they were on the Okehampton road heading towards Redhall Manor.

"So you're going to be guinea pigs for the week?" said Bill.

"That's right. Bella wants to start offering pony camps in the holidays. She's put together an itinerary but wanted to have a trial run before she starts," said Poppy.

"So we're getting a whole week at Redhall absolutely free." Scarlett jiggled in her seat. "I can't wait."

Once they'd pulled into Redhall's immaculately-swept yard Poppy and Scarlett unclipped their seatbelts and went in search of Bella. They found her in the office, staring in exasperation at Harvey Smith, the tabby stable cat named after the famous showjumper, who was stretched across the keyboard of her laptop purring loudly.

"Damn cat. How am I supposed to finish the accounts?" Bella tutted. "Let's get these ponies settled and I'll tell you my plans."

Half an hour later Cloud and Blaze were happily munching hay in their borrowed stables and Poppy and Scarlett had joined their fellow guinea pigs around Bella's large kitchen table.

"I think you all know each other," Bella said, looking at the five expectant faces before her.

The children nodded. Joining Poppy and Scarlett for the week were Bella's grandson, Sam, and two girls from Poppy and Scarlett's school, who also had weekly lessons at Redhall Manor. Tia had brought along her own pony, a chestnut gelding with a white blaze called Rufus, and Niamh would be riding one of the Redhall ponies, a bay mare called Merry. Sam would ride his black Connemara mare Star.

"As you know, some of the children on the pony camps we'll be running will be bringing their own ponies and some will be using ours, so it's a good mix. We'll be hacking out on the moor every morning and having group lessons in the afternoons, tackling a different theme each day, from pole work and jumping to dressage. I'll also be giving lessons on stable management in the evenings. With me so far?"

The children nodded. Bella looked at her watch.

"Today's hack is a six mile circular ride around the base of Barrow Tor. We'll leave at half past ten."

A warm westerly breeze ruffled the ponies' manes and tails as they clip-clopped out of the yard, crossed the road and set off down a rutted track onto the moor. Bella led the way on her liver chestnut Welsh cob Floyd. Tia and Niamh rode two abreast behind her and Poppy, Scarlett and Sam brought up the rear.

Cloud jogged down the track, his neck arched and his tail high.

"He's full of beans," said Bella, looking back. "A blast on the moor will do him good."

Poppy nodded. She could feel excitement zipping through her pony like an electric current. She relaxed into the saddle and kept the lightest touch on his reins until he took her cue and broke into a walk. Bella nodded approvingly.

They followed the track as it climbed steadily, Dartmoor ponies and black-faced sheep watching as they passed. Falling into single file they crossed through a gate onto a rough lane which led past a remote farmhouse, waving to a woman picking runner beans in the garden. Eventually they came to a wide grassy ribbon of a track. Bella pulled Floyd up.

"All OK for a canter?"

"You bet," said Scarlett. Cloud danced on the spot and Poppy tightened her reins.

Bella kicked Floyd on and the cob broke into a canter. Tia and Niamh followed.

"You two go next. I'll bring up the rear," said Sam. Poppy squeezed her legs and Cloud sprang forwards into an easy canter, Blaze following close behind.

"Yee-hah!" shouted Scarlett, waving an imaginary lasso. She was getting so tall she joked that she would soon need roller skates to ride Blaze. This would probably be her last summer riding the big-hearted Dartmoor pony that she'd had since she was five and she was planning to make the most of it. Poppy felt giddy with exhilaration as they sped on.

"Pony camp rocks!" she cried, pushing Cloud faster. She was so focused on Cloud's grey pricked ears that she didn't see the rabbit hole ahead. Neither did Merry. The bay pony's near hind leg shot down the hole and she pitched forwards. There was a gut-wrenching crack and Merry span into a somersault, throwing Niamh into the path of Tia's pony Rufus. Poppy watched with horror as Tia yanked the reins to the right. But it was too late. There was nothing the chestnut gelding could do to avoid Niamh and his hoof landed squarely on the small of her back as she lay face down in the grass.

In the seconds before Scarlett screamed Poppy heard the plaintiff cry of a curlew echo across the moor. *Coor-lee, coor-lee, coor-lee.* And then there was silence.

CHAPTER 2

Poppy, Scarlett and Sam sat on upturned bales of straw outside the tack room listening to Bella's one-sided phone call with growing horror.

"Injured her spine? Are they sure?"

A pause.

"And there's nothing they can do? She could be in a wheelchair for life?"

Scarlett clutched Poppy's hand. They could hear an angry buzz from the other end of the phone.

"Yes, I understand that. But it was an accident. The pony fell down a rabbit hole. There was nothing anyone could have done."

More enraged buzzing, like a mosquito was trapped in the handset.

"I'm so very sorry." Poppy was sure she could detect a catch in Bella's voice. She gripped Scarlett's hand back.

"If there's anything I can do please let me -" Before Bella could finish there was a click. Conversation over, she tramped out of the office, her normally ramrod-straight shoulders stooped, muttering about it being the final straw.

When she saw the three children she cocked her head towards the office. "I expect you heard all that."

They nodded.

"Who was it, Gran?" Sam asked.

"Gordon Cooper."

They looked at her blankly.

"Niamh's dad," Bella said. "He's threatening to sue. Says it should never have happened. I tried to explain it was an accident but he wasn't having any of it. Apparently I should have inspected the route and carried out a risk assessment."

"That's ridiculous!" exploded Scarlett. "Perhaps he'd like to sue the rabbit, too."

"Poor Niamh," said Poppy. "Will she be in hospital for long?"

"A few weeks. And then she'll be transferred to a specialist spinal unit, according to her father. Rufus's hoof damaged her spinal cord. It's unlikely she'll ever walk again."

Scarlett stifled a sob and Poppy put her arm around her shoulders. "We should keep busy. Keep our minds off it. We'll do evening stables tonight, Bella."

Bella rubbed a hand across her face. "That would be a real help, Poppy. There's a million and one things I need to do. Sam'll show you where everything is."

"Do you think your gran'll be alright?" Poppy asked Sam, trying not to look at Merry's empty stable. The police had radioed for a vet once the air ambulance had taken off, its whirring propellers flattening the wiry moorland grasses. The vet slammed the door of his 4x4, strode over to Merry, took one look at her broken leg and shook his head.

"There's nothing I can do. I'm sorry," he told Bella.

She nodded. "Just make it as comfortable for her as possible."

Poppy couldn't bear to watch as the vet sedated the pony.

"Take the horses to the farm. It'll only upset them. I'll come as soon as we're done," Bella said.

Sam took Floyd's reins from his grandmother and they started walking. Poppy glanced back to see Bella rubbing the bay mare's ears, talking to her in a low murmur as the vet reached inside his bag. They were half a mile away when a single gunshot rang out over the moor. Poppy gasped and clung to Cloud's neck. She could hear Scarlett sobbing. Sam's face was like granite.

"She'll be OK. She's as tough as they come," he said now, handing Poppy a pitchfork.

"What did she mean about it being the final straw?"

"A new livery yard opened at Claydon Manor a couple of months ago. State-of-the-art facilities. The horses are stabled in luxury loose boxes and they've got indoor and outdoor schools, a cross country course and a horse walker. They've even got a horse solarium. Gran's already lost two of her best liveries to Claydon and she's worried they won't be the last. That's why she wanted to start the pony camps. She needed the extra income."

"Did you say Claydon Manor?" said Scarlett, poking her head over Floyd's stable door.

Sam nodded.

"But that's -"

"Georgia Canning's home," he said. "According to Gran, they've spent their way through their lottery win and are now having to make the place pay. Georgia's trainer has been promoted to livery yard manager and Georgia's had to sell most of her jumping string to make way for liveries."

"Ouch. I don't suppose that went down too well," said Poppy, remembering Georgia's supercilious smile as she'd beaten Sam and Star in the open class at Redhall's affiliated show the previous autumn.

"And Angela Snell seems intent on poaching Gran's liveries." Sam kicked the bale of hay outside Floyd's stable.

"Who's Angela Snell?" asked Poppy.

"Georgia's trainer. She's a nasty piece of work. She knows she'll be out of a job if the yard isn't a success. And knowing Angela she won't let anything or anybody stand in her way."

That evening, as Poppy cleared the kitchen table and Scarlett began attacking their dirty plates with a soapy washing up brush, Bella asked them if they wanted to leave.

"I've decided to postpone the launch of the pony camps in light of Niamh's accident," she said heavily. "Tia's gone home. I quite understand if you want to go too."

"Are you kidding? We've been looking forward to our week at Redhall for ages," said Scarlett.

"We don't mind that the camp is cancelled. But we'd like to stay and help. That's if you want us to," said Poppy shyly.

Bella looked at Sam, who was flicking through a tattered copy of Horse and Hound.

"It's fine by me. What do you think, Sam?"

He looked up from the magazine and glanced at Poppy. She found her cheeks growing hot.

"Makes sense, now they're here," he said. "We could probably use the help."

"That's settled then." Bella smiled briefly. "You ought to be making a move, Sam. Otherwise your mum'll be moaning about child labour again."

Sam nodded, plucked his cycling helmet from the detritus on the Welsh dresser and headed out of the back door with a casual "See you in the morning". Poppy picked up a tea towel and started drying up, trying to ignore the knowing smile on Scarlett's face.

The phone rang.

"That'll be my insurance broker. I've been trying to reach him all afternoon." Bella picked up the phone, listened for a moment and replaced the handset.

"No luck?" said Poppy.

Bella shook her head. "Wrong number. It's the second one this evening. Leave the rest of the washing up. I'll show you where you're sleeping."

Bella led the two girls to a double bedroom at the front of the house, overlooking the drive. The walls were painted the colour of ripe corn and a reproduction Munnings had been given pride of place above the fireplace. The room was simply furnished - two single beds, a large pine chest of drawers and an old pine door in the wall, which Poppy presumed led to a built-in cupboard - but Bella had added brightly coloured patchwork quilts, scatter cushions and a pile of pony magazines on the chest of drawers.

"What a lovely room," Poppy said.

"The other bedroom is along the landing. I've painted that moss green and there's a Stubbs over the fireplace. That's where Tia and Niamh should have been staying." A look of anguish crossed Bella's face and she sat down on one of the beds. "I can't stop thinking about poor Niamh. If only we'd gone a different way."

Poppy looked at Scarlett helplessly. Bella was usually so indomitable, although Poppy knew her brusque exterior was misleading. She cared deeply about her ponies and riders.

"You mustn't blame yourself. It was an accident," she said. "Niamh's dad'll realise that once he's had a chance to think."

Bella shook her head. "You didn't hear him, Poppy.

He was incandescent. And he holds me wholly responsible." She cocked her ear. "And the blasted phone is ringing again. I suppose I'd better get it."

Once Poppy and Scarlett had unpacked they went down to find Bella. She was sitting at the kitchen table with her head in her hands.

"What's the matter?" said Scarlett.

Bella exhaled slowly. "And there I was thinking that today couldn't get any worse. My Auntie Margaret's had a fall and broken her hip. I need to go and see her."

"That's alright," said Poppy. "You can go in the morning. We'll look after everything here, won't we Scar? Sam can help us."

Scarlett nodded. "Where's she in hospital? Plymouth?"

Bella shook her head. "Inverness."

Poppy and Scarlett were watching an old episode of *Friends* when Bella found them half an hour later.

"It's all sorted," she said. "My godson Scott is going to come and stay for a few days. He's a working pupil at a showjumping yard in Exeter. He used to have a Saturday job here when he was younger and knows the place inside out. I'd cancelled all lessons anyway because of the pony camp, so it's just a matter of looking after the liveries and the riding school ponies. My daughter Sarah - Sam's mum - is also going to move in until I'm back. She's hopeless with horses but she's a wonderful cook and she'll look after you all."

Bella paused. "Do you think you'll be able to cope?"

The two friends nodded.

Bella smiled. "Thank you, girls. I know Redhall will be in good hands."

The next morning Bella lifted her suitcase into the boot of her car, slammed it shut and turned to face Poppy, Scarlett and Sam.

"I've phoned around the liveries and told them what's happening. A couple of them weren't too happy but there's not much I can do about that. The only one I couldn't get hold of is Vivienne. She'll probably be up this afternoon anyway. You'll have to tell her then. Sarah's on her way and Scott said he'd be here by eleven. You've got my number, haven't you Sam?"

He patted the mobile phone in his pocket.

They watched Bella's car disappear down the drive. Poppy was puzzled. Sam had gone quiet the minute Bella had mentioned her godson.

"What's Scott like," she asked.

"He's OK. If you like that sort of thing," he muttered, sweeping his blond fringe out of his eyes.

Scarlett's ears pricked. "And you don't, by the sound of it."

"Let's just say we don't always see eye to eye. But other people seem to like him. Especially girls," he said darkly.

Scarlett raised her eyebrows and winked at Poppy. "He sounds interesting."

CHAPTER 3

Poppy unfolded the list of instructions Bella had pressed into her hand before she'd left. "What should we do first?"

Sam peered over her shoulder. "I'll start on poo-picking if you two can muck out. Do the liveries first, just in case they turn up."

Poppy nodded. Bella's five liveries were all stabled in the newest loose boxes on the south facing side of the yard. She and Scarlett had helped Bella turn them out before breakfast. Two nervy thoroughbreds, one chestnut, one bay. A skewbald, a palomino and a showy Danish warmblood.

Poppy followed Scarlett over to the wheelbarrows, which were propped along the side of the barn, and picked up a pitchfork and broom. They worked together, forking out the muck and wet straw and banking the clean, dry straw around the sides of the stable. While the floors dried they filled the hayracks and water buckets and emptied the wheelbarrows onto Bella's towering muckheap. Poppy was balancing two bales of straw precariously on the wheelbarrow when she heard a car turn into the yard and the sound of a door slamming. As she looked up to see who it was the top bale toppled over and knocked over a bucket of water.

A tall, thin woman wearing pristine white jodhpurs and black leather riding boots strode over and looked down her aquiline nose at Poppy.

"Where's Bella?" she asked in clipped tones.

"I'm sorry, she's not here. Can I help?"

The woman eyed Poppy with disdain. "I don't suppose so for a minute."

"Bella's had to go away for a couple of days," said Scarlett, emerging from the stable behind them.

"Who's running the yard?"

"We are," said Poppy. "With help from Sam and Bella's godson Scott. He works in a showjumping yard in Exeter. He'll be here soon."

The woman's lips grew thin. "I see." She tapped her thigh impatiently. "I wanted to check the farrier's coming this afternoon."

Poppy consulted Bella's instructions.

"John the farrier is due at three o'clock to shoe three of the liveries," she read. "Cherry, Otto and Ariel."

"Make sure he does Ariel first. We have the National Dressage Championships qualifier

19

tomorrow and if my horse hasn't been shod in time there'll be consequences." She looked from Poppy to Scarlett and back again, her eyes narrowed. "Understood?"

Poppy and Scarlett watched the woman stalk back to her car.

"What an old bag," whispered Scarlett, sticking her tongue out at the woman's bony back. Poppy stifled a snort of laughter, quickly disguising it as a cough when she stopped in her tracks and turned back to face them.

"And leave him in the stable in the morning. We've got an early start and the last thing I need is to be traipsing halfway across the paddocks to catch him," she said.

"It'll be a pleasure," Poppy said, hoping the woman didn't detect the irony in her voice.

"That must be Vile Vivienne. Sam warned me about her earlier. He said she orders him about like he's her personal slave," said Scarlett as the woman drove off.

"Which one's Ariel?" Poppy asked.

"The black Danish warmblood that shares a paddock with Paint the skewbald. He's a real sweetie apparently."

"Nothing like his owner then." Poppy blew her fringe out of her eyes. "Let's get this straw down and we'll see how Sam's getting on."

Scarlett produced a penknife from her pocket and cut open the first bale of straw. "What time is Scott supposed to be here?"

Poppy checked her watch.

"Half an hour ago," she said drily.

Poppy and Scarlett were shaking out the last of the straw when a second car pulled into the yard.

"Perhaps that's Scott," said Scarlett hopefully.

But a pretty woman in shorts and a vest top was emerging from the car. Judging by her honey blonde hair she was Sam's mum, Sarah. She saw the two girls and smiled.

"Are you ready for some lunch?"

"Am I ever," said Scarlett.

"Good. I've made a mountain of sandwiches. Mum made me promise to keep you both fed and watered, like you were two of her riding school ponies."

"I'll fetch Sam," Poppy said, heading for the top paddock where she could see the quad bike and trailer Bella used for poo-picking. Sam was in the far corner.

"Your mum's here," she said.

"That's good timing. I've just finished. Want a ride back?" he said. "I'm as safe as houses, honest."

"I guess," said Poppy, looking at the seat of the quad bike dubiously. It didn't look very big.

Sam climbed on and looked around to see where she was. "C'mon then, I'm famished," he said, patting the padded seat behind him.

Poppy gave a tiny shrug and climbed behind him. He turned on the ignition.

"Hold on then," he said, revving the engine. Poppy

held on as loosely as she could and soon they were off, bumping along the field towards the yard. The quad bike hit a rut and lurched sideways. Poppy shrieked, her arms instinctively tightening around Sam. She could feel the muscles in his back flexing as he steered the bike onto more even ground.

"I'll just get rid of this lot on the muck-heap," Sam shouted over his shoulder. He stopped at the gate to the yard and Poppy leapt off like a scalded cat. But not before Scarlett had seen them and had given her a knowing wink.

"Don't," Poppy said. "It was quicker than walking, that's all."

Scarlett smirked. "I'll take your word for it."

They were finishing the last of Sarah's homemade chocolate brownies when the throaty growl of a motorbike cut through the warm afternoon air. Sam checked the time on his phone.

"Only an hour late," he said.

Scarlett rammed the last piece of brownie into her mouth, stood up and ran her hands through her hair. She was already halfway across the yard when a black and silver motorbike roared in. The rider turned off the engine, kicked down the side stand and pulled off his helmet.

"Are you Scott?" said Scarlett, holding out a hand. Instead of shaking it the visitor handed her his helmet.

"I certainly am. And which one of my lovely

helpers are you, Poppy or Scarlett?"

"I'm Scarlett," Scarlett said breathlessly. "We've already mucked out and done the liveries' hay and water and we'll do the riding school ponies after lunch so the only thing you need to do is make sure the farrier does Ariel first because Vile Vivienne's got a dressage qualifier in the morning and she said if he isn't shod there'll be consequences and Bella's had enough consequences this week to last her all year, so we really don't want any more."

Scott threw his head back and laughed loudly. One of his front teeth was chipped, the only flaw in an otherwise perfect smile. "Slow down Scarlett. I have absolutely no idea what you're talking about. Let me have a cup of tea first, eh?"

"Sorry Scott," Scarlett said, bobbing her head. "I'll go and stick the kettle on."

"White, strong and sweet please," he called after her. He gave Sarah a hug and pinched the half-eaten brownie on the paper plate on her lap. She smiled indulgently and batted him on the arm. Sam returned his high-five with about as much enthusiasm as a turkey invited to be guest of honour at lunch on December the twenty-fifth. Poppy allowed herself a small smile. Assuming it was meant for him Scott grinned back.

"And you must be Poppy," he said, his muddy brown eyes assessing her.

She nodded and fled to the kitchen. Scarlett was stirring a mug of builder's tea, a dreamy expression on her face.

"He's so hot," she said. "He looks like Benedict Cumberbatch."

Poppy raised her eyebrows. "D'you think?"

"No, you're right. He's even better looking." Scarlett picked up the mug and headed for the yard. Poppy sighed and followed her.

Scott was lounging against the door to Ariel's stable. Curls of damp hair were stuck to his head and tickled the collar of his battered black leather jacket. When he pulled off his leather gloves to take the tea from Scarlett Poppy noticed his nails were bitten to the quick.

Harvey Smith, woken from his cat bed in the tack room by the roar of the motorbike, padded out, saw Scott and made a beeline for him, rubbing his tabby cheek against Scott's skinny jeans. Scott took a slurp and looked around him.

"It's good to be back," he said.

Scott disappeared inside to unpack and Sarah began tidying away lunch.

"We'd better make a start on the other stables before the farrier gets here," said Sam. "I'll muck out if you two do the hay and water."

Sam worked sparingly and methodically down the line of stables while Poppy and Scarlett emptied wheelbarrows, scrubbed out and filled water buckets and replenished hayracks. Soon the eight stables used by the riding school ponies were finished and it was time to catch the three liveries.

"You bring Ariel and Scarlett and I'll get Cherry and Otto," Sam said, handing Poppy a brand-new leather headcollar. "Just mind Paint because he has a habit of following Ariel out of the gate if you're not careful."

Poppy and Scarlett followed Sam down the dusty track that led to the paddocks. Halfway along he stopped and pointed to a bay mare and a chestnut gelding who were standing nose to tail under an apple tree.

"That's Cherry and Otto," he said. "They've only been with us a few months. They're owned by a husband and wife, Debbie and Tim. They're both a bit highly-strung."

"Cherry and Otto, or Debbie and Tim?" Poppy asked, admiring the two thoroughbreds' fine build and handsome heads.

"They all are actually," said Sam. "Not a good combination. Debbie and Tim are both over-horsed really. They'd only been having lessons for a few months when they bought these two from a yard in Yorkshire that produces top competition horses. They have lessons with Gran but they're both a bit neurotic and worry about absolutely every little thing. They treat Cherry and Otto like their children. There's Ariel, over there."

The big Danish warmblood was watching them from the next paddock. He was a glossy jet black apart from four white socks.

"He's beautiful," Poppy said.

"Much too nice for Vile Vivienne," agreed Scarlett.

Grazing in the far corner of the paddock with his rump towards them was a hogged skewbald cob. Poppy's heart lurched. Paint was a dead ringer for Beau, the horse she'd fallen in love with during her trekking holiday in the Forest of Dean. She opened the gate and walked over to Ariel, offering him a Polo. He lowered his head and took the mint from her palm. She was standing on tiptoes buckling his head strap when she felt a nudge and warm breath on her back. Paint was standing behind her, eying her expectantly.

"Where did you spring from?" she laughed, peeling off a mint for him. He snatched it greedily and nibbled her pocket. "Alright then, just one more. I was saving these for Cloud," she told him.

Poppy clicked her tongue and started leading Ariel towards the gate. Paint pricked his ears and followed. They reached the gate and Poppy looked back. The skewbald cob was so close to Ariel that there was no way she would be able to lead him out without Paint following. She looked around for help but Cherry and Otto's rumps were already disappearing around the corner into the yard. She pushed Paint gently on the shoulder but the sturdy cob simply leant his bulk towards her.

"You're more like Beau than I thought," she told him. "Luckily I know something you won't be able to resist." She peeled off the remaining Polos and dropped the first onto the grass under Paint's nose. Ariel followed her patiently while, one by one, she laid a trail of mints leading away from the gate. As the cob sniffed his way along the trail, snaffling the mints up, Poppy opened the gate and led Ariel through.

"Job done!" she said, patting the black gelding's muscular neck.

By ten to three all three liveries were in their stables ready for the farrier. Poppy picked up a broom and began sweeping the yard. Three o'clock came and went with no sign of John. By a quarter past Sam was anxiously checking the time.

"It's not like him to be late," he said.

"He's probably been held up at his last job. He's not even half an hour late yet," reasoned Poppy.

By half past three Sam's forehead was creased with worry. "It wouldn't normally matter, but if Ariel's not shod today Vivienne will have a nervous breakdown," he said. "Gran must have John's number somewhere. I'll phone him."

As Sam disappeared into Bella's office the phone started ringing.

"That'll be John, letting us know he's running late," said Scarlett.

"What's up?" Poppy asked, as Sam came out shaking his head.

"It was another wrong number. So I tried phoning John, and he said he had a call from Gran cancelling his visit this morning. He's on the other side of Okehampton and won't make it today."

"Why would Bella have cancelled him and not told us? It doesn't make sense," said Scarlett.

"Maybe she forgot about tomorrow's dressage test and thought the farrier would be one less thing for us to worry about," Sam shrugged.

"But he's on the list," said Poppy, pulling it out of her back pocket. "John the farrier at three o'clock to shoe Cherry, Otto and Ariel. Was it definitely Bella who called?"

"That's what John says and he wouldn't have any reason to lie. He's usually really reliable. That's why Gran always has him."

Ariel leant over his stable door and nibbled at Poppy's pony tail. Her face paled.

"Oh God. Who's going to break the news to Vile Vivienne?"

CHAPTER 4

Scott drew the short straw.

"On account of him not being here," said Poppy. "Come on Scar, let's go and tell him the good news."

They found Sarah peeling potatoes in the kitchen.

"Have you seen Scott?" Scarlett asked.

"I've made a bed up for him in Sam's room. He went upstairs to unpack," she said.

As they climbed the stairs they became aware of a soft whistling sound coming from the back of the house.

"Someone's snoring," said Poppy.

"It sounds as if it's coming from Sam's room," whispered Scarlett. "What should we do?"

They stood outside the room and looked at each other uncertainly. The door was ajar. Poppy pushed it open with her index finger and peered around it. There was Scott, fast asleep on top of the duvet in the bed furthest from the door, his shoes still on and his rucksack beside him.

"Dead to the world while we've been hard at it. I thought he was supposed to be here to help," fumed Poppy.

"But we can't wake him. He looks so peaceful," protested Scarlett.

"Too right we can," said Poppy. She coughed loudly. Scott didn't stir. She shoved open the door, letting it hit the wall with a satisfying bang. They watched as Scott opened first one eye, then the other, before yawning so widely they were given an unrivalled view of his tonsils. Puppy pulled a face.

"Sorry to wake you, Scott, but we've got some bad news," said Scarlett.

He sat up, ran a hand through his hair and eyed them blearily.

"Must have just nodded off. Had a late one last night," he said. "What's happened?"

"I'll leave you to fill Scott in," Poppy told Scarlett. "I'm going to see if I can find Vile Vivienne's number. It must be in Bella's office somewhere."

Sam was sitting in Bella's swivel chair with his head in his hands. Poppy stood at the door watching him for a moment. He looked as though he was carrying the weight of the world on his shoulders.

She cleared her throat. Sam looked up and gave her a fleeting smile.

"I'm after Vivienne's phone number. Perhaps Scott can go on a charm offensive and smooth things over," she said brightly.

Sam reached for a blue ledger buried under a pile of Horse and Hound magazines. He flicked through to the back page, copied a phone number on an old envelope and handed it to Poppy.

The phone rang. Sam stared at it as if it was contagious.

"Aren't you going to answer it?" said Poppy.

"What if it's Vile Vivienne? I don't know what to say to her," he said.

Poppy crossed the room and picked up the handset, bracing herself for Vivienne's clipped tones.

"Redhall Manor Equestrian Centre. Can I help?"

But there was nothing but silence on the other end of the line.

"Can I help you?" she repeated.

Poppy held her breath and listened really carefully. Was that static on the line or the sound of someone breathing? A shiver ran down her spine and she stabbed the end call button with her finger. She realised Sam was watching her.

"Wrong number again?" he asked.

"I guess. They didn't actually have the courtesy to say," said Poppy.

"We've had a few this weekend. I'll have to get Gran to call out the engineers when she gets back. She's obviously got a crossed line."

Scott appeared with Scarlett at his heels. Poppy handed him the phone and Vivienne's number.

"Just explain there's been a misunderstanding and

that the farrier has promised to come out first thing tomorrow," said Sam.

Scott nodded at the door. "Clear off you lot. I don't want an audience. There must be plenty of jobs that need doing."

Sam shot Scott a filthy look and Poppy rolled her eyes. Only Scarlett seemed happy to do his bidding.

"I'll go and make you another cup of tea," she said, virtually skipping across the yard. Sam shut the door and beckoned Poppy to follow him down the side of the office to an old window at the end.

"I've got to hear this," he said.

They crouched down under the window and listened as Scott dialled.

"Hello, can I speak to Vivienne Montague? It's Scott from Redhall. I'm afraid I have some bad news. No, Ariel's absolutely fine. It's the farrier. He crashed his van on the way here and won't make it tonight."

Sam shook his head at the bare-faced lie.

"He says he's really sorry and he'll be here at seven tomorrow to shoe Ariel. Will that be in time for your dressage test?"

Poppy held her breath as Vivienne squawked down the line.

"No, there's no point you phoning him. He said he won't be able to get here any earlier. I'll make sure Ariel's groomed and plaited before the farrier arrives if that's any -"

There was a thud. Poppy presumed it was the phone being flung onto the desk. It was followed by the sound of the swivel chair scraping along the flagstone floor and Scott muttering under his breath. Poppy strained to hear. She thought she caught the words "Bloody woman."

Scott threw open the door. Scarlett scampered across the yard and handed him his tea.

"How did it go?" she asked.

"As well as can be expected," he said. "Are you any good at plaiting?"

Poppy checked her watch. Half past four. The stables were mucked out and the hay and water had all been done. The horses had been groomed and were grazing peacefully in their paddocks. There was a natural lull before evening stables. Sam was schooling Star in the indoor school. Scarlett had offered to help Sarah with a supermarket shop and Scott had zoomed off on his motorbike, muttering about needing some down time. Poppy found a sunny corner of the yard and sat down, Harvey Smith purring beside her.

She was texting Caroline when a lorry with a postbox-red cab turned into the Redhall drive, easing its way through the gateposts into the yard with millimetres to spare. The ruddy-faced driver climbed down from the cab, a clipboard in his hands. Poppy slipped her phone into her pocket, hauled herself to her feet and walked over.

"I've got Mrs T's delivery," he said.

Poppy noticed the embroidered logo above the

pocket of his red overalls. *Baxters' Country Store*. Bella hadn't mentioned a delivery on her list.

"Oh, we didn't know you were coming today. I'm not sure where it's supposed to go."

"It's OK, I usually unload it outside the tack room," said the driver. He walked around to the back of the lorry, slid open the doors and reached for a mustard-yellow sack barrow.

"The old girl's really pushed the boat out this week, hasn't she? Enough food to feed the flippin' cavalry and all them fancy supplements. They cost a bleedin' bomb. Has she won the lottery or summat?"

"Er, no." Poppy joined the driver at the back of the lorry and peered inside. "Crikey, is that all for Redhall?"

"Yup."

"Are you sure there hasn't been a mistake?"

The driver whipped a stubby pencil from behind his ear and tapped his clipboard. "It's all on the order form. Just sign here."

Poppy scrawled her signature and the driver began pulling sacks of expensive-looking horse feed onto the sack barrow and wheeling it over to the tack room. Poppy picked up a couple of cartons of liquid pro-biotics and followed him. For the next ten minutes she helped him unload the lorry. Supplements for healthy bones and joints, strong hooves and glossy coats. Antioxidants and draughts to aid gastric health and digestion. Herbal tinctures promising vitality. Who knew all this stuff even existed? And since when had Bella, an old-school equestrian, had her head turned by all the marketing hype?

Once they had finished unloading the lorry Poppy sat on a tub of herbs for hormonal mares and watched it reverse slowly out of the drive. She was just finishing her text to Caroline when Sam led Star out of the indoor school and did a double take.

"What on earth's all that?"

"It's Bella's delivery from Baxters'. The driver said he usually leaves it outside the tack room."

"It can't be. This is way too much. Gran has about a fifth of this. And none of this expensive stuff." He picked up a tub and read the label. "'Electrolyte supplement for the performance horse.' I don't even know what it is. And look at the price - nearly twenty quid! Gran hasn't ordered this."

Poppy felt the colour drain from her face. "But it was all on the order form, Sam. The man from Baxters' showed me before I signed for it. Bella must have changed the order."

"You signed for it?" Sam's eyebrows shot up. "This is going to cost hundreds of pounds. There's no way Gran can afford it, especially at the moment."

"I'm sorry," Poppy said in a small voice. "I thought I was doing the right thing. I should have come and found you."

"It's not your fault. I'll phone Baxters' now. Explain there's been some sort of a mix-up. I'm sure they'll sort it out."

"I'll do Star," she offered.

Sam handed her Star's reins and Poppy led the mare over to the tie ring outside her stable.

"I feel terrible," she whispered as she untacked Star and ran a body brush over her gleaming coat. The mare whickered as Sam tramped over from Bella's office.

"Any luck?" Poppy asked.

He shook his head. "They have an exchange policy on tack and rugs, but not on food." He rested his head on Star's flank and stared at the mountainous pile of feed and supplements. "Looks like we're stuck with it."

After dinner Poppy took a mug of hot chocolate and a carrot out to the yard, her eyes on Cloud's borrowed stable. She whistled softly and his head appeared over the stable door. He watched her cross the yard, his silver grey ears pricked. She offered him the carrot and he crunched it noisily while she opened the stable door and settled in the straw to drink her hot chocolate.

She still felt bad about the Baxters' order, although Sam had told her not to blame herself. If only she had checked with him before she'd signed the order form. She had offered to use her savings to buy half a dozen of the tubs of supplements, joking that she would have the shiniest, calmest, least hormonal gelding with the healthiest digestive system and hooves ever seen. But Sam had told her not to be silly and that Bella would sort it all out when she was back.

"And I haven't spent any time with you today, have I Cloud?" she said, kissing his nose. "It's just been manic." It was true. She had hardly stopped. Her back and shoulders ached from hefting bales of straw and wheelbarrows of muck and despite five minutes spent scrubbing with a nail brush until the tips of her fingers were pink her nails were still black with grime. And tomorrow it would start all over again.

"Whoever says that working with horses is easy should give it a try for a few days. It's like painting the Forth Bridge." Cloud nuzzled Poppy's hand, which still smelt enticingly of carrots. She scratched his forehead. "It takes so long that by the time you've finished you have to start all over again."

Realising Poppy didn't have any more titbits, Cloud sank to the floor and lay down in the straw. Poppy snuggled up close and sighed contentedly.

"We'll try and get out for a ride tomorrow," she promised him. "Just you and me."

Poppy was letting herself in the back door when the phone started ringing. When no-one answered she picked up the extension in the kitchen, expecting another wrong number. She almost jumped out of her skin when Vile Vivienne began screeching down the phone.

"I phoned the farrier and there was no crash! He said Bella cancelled his visit. Well, she had no right. I have been working towards tomorrow's qualifier for the last six months. Six months! And she's ruined my chances. But worse than that, I have been lied to. I will put up with a lot, but I will not tolerate lying. I shall be removing Ariel from the yard."

"But -" began Poppy.

"And in the light of what's happened I consider my contract with Redhall to be null and void. I will not be giving one month's notice. Please have him ready at ten o'clock in the morning."

The line went dead. With a sinking heart Poppy headed for the lounge to break the bad news.

CHAPTER 5

Poppy woke early to the chatter of magpies. She squinted at her watch. Ten to five. She closed her eyes and tried to empty her brain so she could drift back into unconsciousness. But a shaft of sunlight that had slunk through a crack in the curtains like a cat burglar flitting through a heavily-alarmed art gallery played on her eyelids, banishing any chance of sleep.

Sighing, Poppy threw off her duvet and grabbed a clean teeshirt and pair of jodhpurs from her case. As she did she glanced at Scarlett. Her best friend's auburn hair was fanned around her face, her duvet was tucked under her chin and she was breathing deeply. She didn't look like she would be waking up anytime soon.

Poppy picked an apple from the fruit bowl and scribbled a note on an old envelope. *Gone for a ride. Will be back by seven.* She found her jodhpur boots in the tangle of wellies and riding boots by the back door and went in search of her pony.

Cloud must have had a sixth sense. When Poppy burst out of the back door, the apple between her teeth, he was watching over his stable door as if he'd been expecting her. He whickered and she scratched behind his ear, took a last bite of apple and gave him the rest.

Poppy reached under the flowerpot brimming with pale pink geraniums for the key to the tack room, plonked her hat on her head and carried Cloud's saddle and bridle to his stable. He shook his head impatiently as she tacked him up. Blaze, Star, the riding school ponies and the liveries all watched with interest as she led the Connemara over to the mounting block, tightened his girth, pulled down his stirrups and swung into the saddle. Soon they were turning out of the yard towards the moor.

They crossed the road outside the riding school and followed the rutted track they'd ridden along on Bella's first fateful trek to Barrow Tor. So much had happened since the accident it seemed like another life, yet it was only two days ago. An unwelcome memory of Merry pitching forwards as her hind leg disappeared down the rabbit hole swam in front of Poppy's eyes and she shook it away. The last thing she wanted to do was re-live that terrible morning. Instead she fixed her eyes on Cloud's pricked grey ears and tried to forget.

Ahead an orange sun smouldered behind the

purple and grey horizon. Behind her the moon was fading in the early morning sky like a footprint in wet sand. The air smelt fresh, cold and clean and Poppy breathed deeply. Gradually she felt the tension of the last forty-eight hours ease from her shoulders. Her thoughts turned to Scott. Scarlett seemed in awe of Bella's godson but Poppy had been relieved to discover within minutes of meeting him that she was totally immune to his charms. He was way too smooth for her liking. And his laidback attitude to his new responsibilities irritated her. He was supposed to be helping, yet he'd barely lifted a finger while the rest of them worked their socks off to keep the yard running like clockwork. And she hated the way he belittled Sam.

Sam had got his own back the night before. As they'd sat down to eat Sarah's legendary fish pie, Scarlett had asked Scott how he'd chipped his front tooth.

Scott had run his tongue along the offending tooth and given them a rueful smile.

"An argument with a feisty gelding," he said mysteriously.

"At the showjumping yard in Exeter?" Scarlett asked, impressed.

Sam snorted with laughter and Scott shot him a filthy look.

"Not exactly. He fell off Treacle," Sam smirked.

"Our Treacle?" said Poppy. She couldn't imagine Scott atop the diminutive Welsh pony that Bella used

41

for Redhall's beginners, despite his uncanny knack of dumping most of them in the nearest puddle while they were out on a hack. With a stomach the size of a barrel and an evil glint in his eye, the chestnut Section A gelding shared more than a passing resemblance to a Thelwell pony and was definitly not as sweet as his name suggested. It was a wonder the beginners came back for more.

"I was eight at the time," Scott clarified. "I learnt to ride on him. And he can buck like a bronco when he's in the mood, you know."

"That's funny, I never had a problem with him," said Sam, looking more cheerful than he had all day.

Cloud reached the gate at the top of the track. Ahead was the lane that led to the farmhouse where Poppy had called for help. A bridleway to the right led back down to the riding school. Poppy's stomach rumbled and she checked her watch. Half past six. She turned him right.

"Come on Cloud, let's go and get some breakfast."

Poppy fed Cloud and Blaze and followed the smell of bacon that was wafting from the open kitchen window. As she heeled off her jodhpur boots by the back door a white van pulled into the yard. A woman wearing a royal blue apron let herself out of the driver's side and went around to the back of the van. Poppy pulled her boots back on and wandered over. Painted on the side in a curly script decorated with denim blue forget-me-knots were the words *Fern's*

Flowers.

The woman in the apron appeared holding a huge bouquet of white lilies.

"These are for Bella Thompson," she said.

"They're beautiful," said Poppy. "She's not here at the moment but I can take them."

The woman handed Poppy the bouquet. The scent they gave was cloying and Poppy rubbed her nose with the back of her hand to head off a sneeze.

"There's a card in with them," said the woman, pointing to a small white envelope tucked between the stalks. She smiled sympathetically. "I'm sorry for your loss."

What a strange thing to say, Poppy thought, as she carried the flowers into the kitchen. Sarah was standing by Bella's massive range cooker frying bacon.

"Flowers?" she asked, surprised.

"They're for Bella," Poppy said. She fished around for the envelope and handed it to Sarah.

"Perhaps Mum's got an admirer," Sarah joked. "I'm sure she won't mind me having a look to see who they're from."

She used the bread knife to open the envelope and took out a card with a dove on the front. The knife slipped through her fingers and clattered to the floor. Her hand flew to her mouth.

"What's wrong?"

"It can't be right. They must have delivered them to the wrong address," she said.

"The *Ferns Flowers* woman definitely said it was for

Bella. Why, what does the card say?"

"RIP," said Sarah faintly.

Poppy's mind went blank. "What does that stand for?"

"Rest in Peace," said Sarah with a shiver.

"That's what people say when someone's died, isn't it?" said Scarlett, as they waited for Vile Vivienne to arrive to take Ariel to his new home.

Poppy nodded. "Sarah was a bit freaked out at first, and then she wondered if someone in the village had heard about her Great Auntie Margaret's fall and jumped to the wrong conclusion."

Scarlett looked sceptical. "What, like Chinese whispers? Sounds unlikely to me."

"That's what I thought, too," said Poppy.

At ten o'clock on the dot a familiar-looking smart sky blue lorry pulled into the yard.

Poppy watched glumly from Paint's stable as Vile Vivienne jumped out of the passenger door and strode over to the office, her lips pursed. Another woman let herself out of the driver's side and began letting down the ramp. Poppy wracked her brains, trying to remember where she'd seen the lorry before. And then she noticed a small navy logo on the passenger door and groaned.

Vivienne emerged from the office with Scott trailing behind her.

"Are you sure I can't persuade you to stay?" he said half-heartedly.

Vivienne waved him away with her hand. "My mind is made up. I've been considering a move to Claydon Manor for a while. The facilities there put this place to shame. I only stayed out of misguided loyalty to Bella. But I will not be lied to. Fortunately Angela was more than happy to offer me a place."

I bet she was, thought Poppy, watching Georgia Canning's former instructor fix partitions in the horse lorry. She walked down the ramp and looked around, unimpressed. She had cold grey eyes and a contemptuous look on her face, as if she had a permanent bad smell under her nose.

"Where's the horse?" she asked, looking around disdainfully.

Vile Vivienne pointed to Ariel's stable. His noble head appeared over the stable door and Vivienne's normally arch expression softened. She may be an old dragon but she does love him, Poppy realised.

Sam appeared with Ariel's tack and grooming kit while Scarlett ran into the tack room to find his rugs. Soon the big black gelding had been loaded onto the lorry and it had pulled onto the Okehampton road bound for Tavistock.

"Good riddance," said Scott. "That woman was as mad as a box of frogs if you ask me."

"She also paid through the nose for Gran's deluxe bespoke livery package. And now she's gone. And to Claydon Manor of all places," said Sam.

"Chill out Samantha," mocked Scott.

"Vivienne may have been vile, but she and Ariel

have been here for years. Perhaps you'd like to phone Gran and let her know her oldest livery has gone." He shoved his hands into his pockets. "Actually don't bother. I'd rather break the news to her myself when she gets back from Great Auntie Margaret's. Just try not to lose us any more liveries will you?"

"I don't know why he's so uptight," said Scott as Sam stomped over to the trailer, hooked it onto the quad bike and roared off towards the top paddocks.

Poppy stared at him in disbelief. "Because he's worried about Redhall's future!" she spluttered. "Angela Snell has poached so many of Bella's liveries she's struggling to keep the place afloat. That's why she decided to start trekking holidays. But that's on hold after Niamh's accident. No wonder Sam's upset."

Was that a glimmer of uncertainty flickering across Scott's face? Poppy wasn't convinced. But as she pushed the wheelbarrow towards the hay barn she hoped he might have finally got the message that all was not well at Redhall.

CHAPTER 6

Poppy and Scarlett were fluffing up the straw bed in Paint's stable when Sam appeared with three headcollars.

"Where's Scott?" he asked.

"He went in to make us a cup of tea," said Scarlett.

"Really? I don't think I've ever known him to make a drink for anyone other than himself," said Sam.

"Yes, but he did disappear about half an hour ago. He's probably fast asleep on the sofa by now," said Poppy.

"It's hardly surprising. He must work so hard at that showjumping yard," said Scarlett.

Poppy and Sam exchanged a look.

"I could do with some help exercising the liveries. Fancy coming with me?"

Scarlett's eyes lit up. "You get to ride the liveries?"

Sam nodded. "Debbie and Tim pay extra for

Cherry and Otto to be exercised a couple of times a week. So does Kim, Ellie's owner. Sometimes Gran lunges them, sometimes I school them, but I reckon we deserve an hour off to go for a hack, don't you?"

"Bags I ride Cherry," said Scarlett.

"I'd better take Otto. He can be a bit unpredictable." Sam held out a navy headcollar for Poppy. "Are you OK with Ellie?"

Poppy nodded. Ellie was a showy palomino mare with four white socks and an extravagantly long mane and forelock. At 15.2hh she was a hand taller than Cloud but more finely-built.

"Her name's actually Elidi, which means gift of the sun in Greek," said Sam as Poppy tied Ellie up next to Otto. "She's not a novice ride, but I reckon you can handle her."

The mare fidgeted while Poppy set to work brushing the dust from her butterscotch-coloured coat. She tossed her head as Poppy combed her mane and pawed the ground impatiently when Poppy appeared with her tack.

Poppy placed the saddle on the mare's back, buckled the girth loosely, looped the headcollar around Ellie's neck and put the bridle on. As she fastened the noseband Harvey Smith darted out of the tack room door and flashed across the yard with his tabby tail as bushy as a fox's, sending an empty bucket flying. Ellie leapt about a foot in the air, her hooves jangling on the concrete yard.

"Easy girl," Poppy murmured, running her hand

along Ellie's neck. She felt a flutter in her stomach at the thought of riding the flighty mare.

Scarlett was already leading Cherry over to the mounting block. Poppy re-tied her ponytail, put on her hat, unfastened Ellie's headcollar and waited while Scarlett mounted the towering thoroughbred.

"It's about two degrees cooler up here," Scarlett grinned. "Blaze is going to feel like a Shetland pony after Cherry."

Poppy tightened Ellie's girth, adjusted the stirrup leathers and led her over to the mounting block. She climbed the steps, gathered the reins in her left hand and was just about to put her left foot in the stirrup when the mare swung her quarters away, leaving a yawning gap between them. Poppy got back down, circled the mare and led her back to the mounting block. But she did exactly the same again, swinging away just as Poppy was about to get on.

"Having a spot of bother?" said a voice. Poppy turned to see Scott lounging against the post and rail fence around the school, his hands curled around a mug of tea.

Poppy felt her face grow hot. "Third time lucky," she muttered, circling Ellie again. This time the mare backed away from the mounting block before Poppy had even climbed onto it.

"I'll hold her for you if you like," Scott said, not waiting for an answer. He took Ellie's reins and pushed her rump firmly towards the mounting block. He scratched the mare's poll and she lowered her head demurely and stood perfectly still while Poppy jumped on and gathered her reins.

Ellie nibbled Scott's pockets and sniffed at the dregs of his tea. Poppy wouldn't have been surprised if she'd fluttered her long eyelashes at him. The palomino mare had obviously fallen for his charms, too.

"Thanks," she said.

"Anytime. Enjoy your ride."

"The buckets and water troughs need filling," Sam said as they rode out of the yard. Scott pulled a face and disappeared into Bella's office.

"If they're done by the time we get back I'll eat my hat," Sam sighed.

Ellie jogged up the road behind Otto and Cherry, her nostrils flared as she spooked at the tattered remains of a plastic carrier bag caught on a barbed wire fence. Poppy grabbed a handful of her long mane and held on tight.

"It's alright, you silly horse. It's a bag, not a bogeyman. It won't hurt you."

In the year since she'd learnt to ride on Flynn, Scarlett's brother Alex's rotund Dartmoor pony, Poppy had only ever ridden four other horses. Cloud, Bella's New Forest mare Rosie, Sam's Connemara Star and Beau, the big, hairy piebald cob she'd fallen in love with during their week at Oaklands Trekking Centre in the Forest of Dean. Ellie was nothing like any of them. She felt like an active volcano, ready to erupt at any minute.

Sam pulled Otto alongside her.

"Alright?" he asked.

Poppy licked her lips. The roof of her mouth was sandpaper dry. "She's quite, er, lively," she said, as Ellie shied at a sheep, cannoning into Otto before Poppy could stop her.

"She's always a bit spooky when she hasn't been out for a few days. She'll settle down in a minute," he said.

"I'll take your word for it," Poppy muttered, tightening her reins.

Instead of turning onto the track Poppy and Cloud had followed that morning, Sam took a right into a narrow lane that ran parallel to a stream. A clutch of fluffy yellow mallard ducklings glided gracefully after their parents. Poppy imagined their tiny feet paddling furiously under the water and smiled.

"OK for a trot?" Sam called.

"You bet!" cried Scarlett.

Ellie needed no encouragement either and sprang into the floatiest trot Poppy had ever experienced. It felt as though they were trotting on air.

They reached a T-junction and turned right over an old stone bridge. Ellie spooked, boggle-eyed, at a yellow salt bin, but this time Poppy was ready for her and sat relaxed in the saddle.

"We usually have a canter through the woods," said Sam, turning Otto down a bridleway. Ellie snatched at her bit and crabbed sideways down the track, but

Poppy was unperturbed. She'd realised that nothing the mare did was malicious, she was just fresh. And Poppy had to admit her canter was as amazing as her trot. They cantered through the woods, one after the other, the horses' pounding hooves sending pheasants scurrying for cover.

Too soon they'd reached the end of the bridleway and turned for home.

"This road brings us out at the back of Gran's. We can ride through the fields back to the yard," said Sam.

Ten minutes later they came to a five bar gate.

Ellie gawked at a puddle of water.

"That's funny," Poppy said.

"What is?" asked Scarlett.

"Look at that massive puddle. But I can't remember the last time it rained, can you?"

Scarlett shrugged. "Perhaps it rained last night."

They rode past the field Cloud was sharing with Blaze and Treacle. Poppy held her hand over her face.

"What on earth are you doing?" said Sam.

"Hiding from Cloud. I don't want him to see me riding another horse," Poppy whispered. At that moment Cloud lifted his grey head and whinnied. "Oh no, he's seen me!" she cried.

Scarlett howled with laughter. "What, are you worried he'll be jealous? He's a *horse*!"

Scott was sitting on a bale of hay texting on his phone when they arrived back in the yard, a row of empty water buckets at his feet.

"I might have known," muttered Sam, jumping off Otto.

Scott shoved his phone in his back pocket. "Good ride?"

"It was great. Cherry's just brilliant. I've decided I want my next pony to be a 16.2hh thoroughbred. I'm going to skip the 14.2hh stage," said Scarlett.

Scott noticed Sam scowling at the empty water buckets. "Before you say anything, Samantha, I did try and fill them, but there's no water."

"What do you mean?"

Scott sauntered across to the tap outside the tack room and turned the handle. The tap coughed, gurgled and spluttered out a few paltry drops of water.

"See? I've told your mum. She doesn't know where the stopcock is so she's trying to get through to Bella, but it's just going straight to answerphone at the moment."

Poppy tied Ellie up and began untacking her. "It might be a leak. Remember that puddle we passed on the way in? I could phone the water board. They might send someone out to have a look."

"In the meantime where on earth are we going to get water for the horses?" said Scarlett.

She had a point, thought Poppy. The nearest neighbour was probably a quarter of a mile away. She remembered the family of mallards.

"What about the stream? It's a bit of a trek but if

we do it together it shouldn't be too bad. At least the water is clean and fresh."

"Sounds like our only option," said Sam. "I'll turn Ellie out if you phone the water board, Poppy. There should be a number in the office somewhere."

Harvey Smith was sprawled over Bella's dog-eared phone book. Poppy tickled his chin and deposited him on the floor. He immediately jumped onto her lap and began kneading her thighs, purring loudly. Poppy flicked through the phone book to W and there was the number she was looking for in Bella's precise handwriting.

She was just about to pick up the phone and dial when it rang, making her jump. Harvey Smith mewed crossly and sprang off her lap.

"Hello?"

Poppy listened for an answer but all she could hear was static.

"Can I help you?"

Still no answer. Poppy felt irritation rise. This wasn't crossed lines. Someone was deliberately phoning Redhall and giving them the silent treatment, she was sure of it.

"Look, if you're the person who keeps calling, I think you've got the wrong number. You need to check it and stop phoning this one. It's getting really annoying," she said.

She nearly jumped out of her skin when a bark of bitter laughter rang in her ear.

"Who *is* this?" she said.

But the laughter had been replaced by the drone of the ring tone. Whoever it was had hung up.

Poppy found the others stacking buckets ready to carry them down to the stream.

"The water board is going to send someone out in the morning. They say if no-one has turned off the stopcock it's probably a leak. And since none of us know where the stopcock is, they're probably right," she said. "Oh, and there was another nuisance call, though this time I heard someone laughing. And when I dialled 1471 it was number withheld."

"I took one before breakfast," said Scarlett. "It's a bit creepy, isn't it? Do you think someone's trying to freak us out?"

Scott's face was scornful. "They'll have to try harder than that."

CHAPTER 7

Poppy collapsed in an exhausted heap in the shade of an apple tree. Opposite her a pink-faced Scarlett was grimacing as she stretched out her back.

"I'm so sweaty," she moaned.

"Horses sweat," Poppy corrected her. "Men perspire and ladies *glow*."

"Well, I'm glowing like a lightbulb at the moment. I'm shattered."

It had taken the four of them a solid two hours of back-breaking work to fill all the water troughs and buckets. The stream had seemed a lot closer when they'd ridden past it. In fact it was a ten minute walk there and even longer on the way back with heavy buckets bumping against their shins and water sloshing all over their feet.

While Poppy had hefted buckets she'd mulled over the last couple of days and she had come to the conclusion that the series of unfortunate events to befall Redhall was no coincidence.

"Scar, I think someone's trying to sabotage the riding school," she blurted out.

"What do you mean?"

"I know it sounds far-fetched but think about it. The nuisance calls. The delivery from Baxters' that no-one ordered. The lilies. Someone called the farrier to tell him not to come and it wasn't Bella."

"I think your imagination's gone into overdrive. Who on earth would want to harm the riding school?"

"It's obvious isn't it? Who's in direct competition with Redhall? Who's going to benefit if Bella goes out of business?"

Scarlett gawped at her. "You don't mean -?"

"Yes, I do," said Poppy. "Angela Snell."

They heard the click of a gate. Sam was walking towards them with a couple of cans of lemonade.

"Don't say anything yet," Poppy whispered to Scarlett. "We need to get some hard evidence before we accuse her of anything."

"How on earth are we going to do that?"

Poppy grinned. "Fancy a trip to Claydon Manor?"

"But how will we get there?"

"There are a couple of old bikes at the back of the hay barn. We'll ask Sarah if we can borrow them. And we'll go this evening."

Poppy found Sarah in the kitchen stirring a huge saucepan of bolognese sauce. She glanced at the clock above the sink. "It'll only be another twenty minutes," she said.

"It smells yummy. Sarah, you know those two old bikes in the barn?"

Sarah smiled. "I certainly do. They were mine and my brother's. Why?"

"Scarlett and I wondered if we could go on a bike ride on them after dinner."

Sarah dipped a teaspoon into the sauce, tasted it and added a pinch of oregano. "You don't have any cycling helmets."

"We could wear our riding hats," Poppy said.

"Alright. As long as you promise to stick to the lanes and be back before it gets dark."

"I knew I shouldn't have had seconds, but Sarah's such a good cook. Her spaghetti was to die for. And now I'm absolutely stuffed," groaned Scarlett.

They pushed the two mountain bikes out of the barn. Poppy wheeled hers past Cloud's stable and peered in. He was pulling wisps of hay from his hayrack.

"Hey baby," she called softly. He abandoned the hay and came over to say hello. She breathed in his familiar scent and sighed.

"I wish I could stay here with you all evening, Cloud, but I've got to go. Things to do, people to see," she told him, kissing his nose. He nudged her and returned to his hay.

"I used to pretend my first bike was a pony," she

told Scarlett. "I used to practice my rising trot as I cycled round and round the park near our house. And when we got home I would poke handfuls of grass into the handlebars and offer it a bucket of water."

Scarlett hooted with laughter. She looked down at Sarah's rusted pink Raleigh. "Let's pretend these are famous horses. It'll make the ride much more fun. Bags mine is Red Rum."

"Hello Black Beauty," Poppy said, patting the coal black frame of her bike. She clicked her tongue and pedalled off, Scarlett in close pursuit.

"Trot on," Poppy shouted in her best riding instructor's voice. "On the left diagonal please, Scarlett. That's it. Up down, up down."

The two friends circled the yard, their bikes wobbling dangerously as they bobbed up and down. Horses heads appeared over stable doors as they careered past. Poppy was giggling so hard her insides ached.

"Come on Beauty," she cried, pedalling as fast as she could. "Let's race Red Rum to Claydon Manor!"

Twenty minutes later the two girls pulled onto the verge opposite a pair of grand wrought iron gates set in an imposing stone wall. To the right was a keypad on a metal post and set into the stone was a slate sign saying *Claydon Manor*.

"Electronic gates," said Scarlett.

"And CCTV," said Poppy, nodding towards a small camera on top of one of the huge gate posts.

"How are we going to get in?"

Poppy reached into her backpack and pulled out a royal blue book.

"I found Ariel's equine passport in Bella's office. I'm amazed Angela Snell didn't ask for it when they picked him up. Perhaps she's not quite as efficient as we think. We'll say Sam sent us over with it."

Scarlett looked impressed. "Ingenious. Perhaps I'd better let you do the talking."

"There's a first time for everything," Poppy teased. "C'mon, let's press the buzzer."

They wheeled their bikes across the road and Poppy studied the keypad. "I guess it's the one with the bell on," she said, jabbing it with her index finger.

A tinny voice made them jump. "Who is this?"

Poppy cleared her throat. "It's, um, Poppy and Scarlett from Redhall. Sam sent us over. We've got Ariel's passport."

An exasperated sigh emanated from the keypad and the gates clicked and began to swing open.

"You'd better come in," said the voice.

Poppy and Scarlett pushed their bikes towards a beautiful grey stone Georgian manor house. Poppy's eyes were on stalks as she took in the sleek thoroughbreds grazing in immaculate paddocks on either side of the sweeping gravelled drive.

"Wow," she said. "This is some place."

"Don't forget it was all down to a winning lottery ticket," said Scarlett, waving her hand dismissively. "They didn't earn it. They just got lucky."

A figure was beckoning them from a stable block to the right of the house. Even from this distance Poppy recognised the prickly demeanour of Angela Snell.

"So what are we looking for?" Scarlett asked.

Poppy shrugged. "I'm not really sure. Anything that might link Snell or the Cannings to what's been happening at Redhall, I suppose."

They set their bikes against a granite wall and walked over to Angela Snell. The livery yard manager held her hand out. Poppy gave her the passport.

"Thanks," said Angela curtly. "I thought Vivienne had it."

A whinny rang out across the cobbled yard.

"It's Ariel," said Poppy. "Can we say a quick hello?"

Angela Snell sighed. "Just a quick one. I have work to do."

The black gelding seemed pleased to see them and delicately ate the Polo Scarlett offered him.

"Nice loose box," said Poppy, noticing the rubber matting, automatic water drinker and thick bed of shavings. "There's even a smoke alarm. No wonder Vile Vivienne wanted to move him here."

Angela strode across the yard, checking her watch. "All done?"

"Is Georgia around?" asked Scarlett.

"Why, are you friends?" said Angela, surprised. Her eyes travelled over Scarlett's dishevelled appearance with barely disguised contempt.

"Not friends exactly," said Scarlett, unperturbed.

"We used to go to the same school. When Georgia and her mum and dad still lived in a three bedroomed semi in Tavistock and the family car was a clapped out hatchback."

Poppy's eyes were drawn to the pristine white Range Rover parked in the furthest corner of the yard next to a silver Bentley. It was impossible to imagine the family who owned all this ever having to make do with a clapped out hatchback.

"She's schooling Barley in the indoor arena," Angela said.

"I'm sure she won't mind us watching," said Scarlett, dragging Poppy towards the huge wooden-slatted building behind the row of loose boxes before Angela could stop her.

"Trust Georgia to have an indoor *arena*," she muttered.

Poppy recognised the palomino gelding Georgia was cantering in perfect twenty metre circles at the far end of the arena.

"He's the one Georgia beat Sam on, isn't he?" she said.

Scarlett nodded. "He's her top jumping pony. Her mum paid over ten thousand pounds for him. He's a demon against the clock."

"Not as fast as Star though," said Poppy, remembering how Sam had only lost to Georgia because Barley had rattled a pole which had fallen during Sam's round.

Georgia changed reins and the palomino executed a

flawless flying change. As she cantered towards them she noticed them watching and eased Barley into a trot. She stared at them with china blue eyes.

"I recognise you. You were at the Redhall affiliated show last summer. You're Sam's fan club. What are you doing here?" she said.

Scarlett scowled and was about to say something but Poppy cut across her. "Angela told us to come and say hello. We've just dropped off Ariel's passport."

Georgia patted her pony's neck and slid off. She was wearing a crimson polo shirt, cream jodhpurs and expensive-looking leather boots the same shade of bitumen black as her plaited hair. Her high cheekbones and English rose complexion made Poppy think of Snow White. Without the seven dwarfs of course. Although Angela would make a convincing Evil Queen.

"Nice place you've got here, Georgia. It puts Redhall to shame," Poppy said.

Scarlett's eyes widened but Poppy winked at her and she took the hint.

"It's amazing," she agreed. "We'd love a guided tour. If you've got time."

Georgia looked at them warily. Poppy held her breath. They needed evidence that Angela Snell was trying to sabotage Redhall and if being nice to stuck-up Georgia Canning was the only way they were going to get it, it was a price worth paying. She smiled at Georgia hopefully.

"OK," Georgia shrugged. "I'll just put Barley away first." She led the palomino gelding to a row of looseboxes opposite Ariel's.

"How many liveries do you have?" asked Poppy.

"Ten with Ariel. Plus my ponies, Barley and Fizz."

"You used to have way more than two didn't you?" said Scarlett.

Georgia gave a brief nod and began untacking Barley. Poppy studied the girl's expression for clues but her face gave nothing away. Yet something about her was different. Poppy thought back to the day of the Redhall show. When Georgia had ridden past Poppy had been struck by her hooked Roman nose, the only imperfection in an otherwise flawless face. But as she watched Georgia undo Barley's girth and run up the stirrup leathers she realised the Roman nose had gone, smoothed away by a surgeon's knife.

Georgia led them to the largest tack room Poppy had seen in her life. It looked like a high-end tack shop, with rows of gleaming saddles and bridles and piles of neatly-folded day rugs, night rugs and New Zealand rugs. The room smelt of saddle soap and hoof oil.

"Each livery has their own storage trunk where they keep their grooming kits. Every horse has a daily groom as part of the service," said Georgia. "And this is the feed room."

Poppy and Scarlett followed her into an adjoining room which contained huge bins of food.

"You must get through tons of feed with twelve

horses. Where do you get it from," asked Scarlett conversationally.

"Baxters'," said Georgia. "They do a monthly delivery."

Poppy gasped as Scarlett elbowed her sharply in the ribs. Fortunately Georgia had already turned away.

"This is the solarium," she said, opening the double doors of a high-ceilinged barn. "We have two heat lamps so two horses can use it at once."

Poppy cricked her neck to examine the space-age bulbs set in curved units above two empty stalls. "What do they do that the sun can't?" she asked, genuinely curious.

"The lamps have infra-red rays that help increase blood circulation and muscle elasticity, which can help reduce healing time for injuries. We also use them for drying horses after a bath, especially in the winter." Georgia sounded as if she was reading from a brochure. She flicked a switch on the wall and the lamps in the solarium nearest to them glowed orange. "And they're nice and warm to sit under when you're cleaning your tack."

"You clean your own tack?" asked Scarlett in disbelief.

Georgia shot her a scornful look. "Who else do you think does it?"

She switched off the solarium and stalked over to a huge metal contraption which reminded Poppy of an industrial-sized rotary washing line.

"This is the horse walker. All the horses have

weekly solariums and are exercised daily, either by Angela or me or on the horse walker."

"Wouldn't they prefer to go out for a hack?" said Scarlett. Poppy gave her a warning look. They were supposed to be keeping Georgia on side after all.

Georgia shrugged. "Probably. But owners expect us to have one for the price they're paying."

"Do you have any vacancies at the moment?" asked Poppy.

"Why? Think you can afford it here?"

Poppy shook her head and kept her face neutral, although inside she was seething. "I prefer to keep my pony at home, thanks. I just wondered."

"Whatever," said Georgia. "We have two at the moment. The two looseboxes next to Ariel. Though Angela is confident they'll be filled very shortly."

They walked back to the yard. Behind the palatial Georgian mansion the sun was setting.

"Thanks for showing us around. It was very *interesting*, although I don't think my pony Blaze would like it here," said Scarlett.

Georgia stared at her. "I used to know a pony called Blaze. She was the first pony I ever rode. She was owned by the daughter of a friend of my mother's. They lived on a ramshackle farm in Waterby."

"We still do," Scarlett said quietly.

"I *thought* I recognised you at the Redhall show but you said we'd never met before." Georgia's cut-glass accent sounded unnecessarily loud.

"We used to go to the same school a long time ago. Before you had all *this*," Scarlett said, with a sweep of her arm.

There was an awkward silence. Poppy could feel Scarlett bristling beside her and gave her a nudge.

"Come on Scar, we'd better make a move. There aren't any lights on the bikes and we promised Sarah we'd be home before it gets dark."

Scarlett nodded, turned on her heels and headed for the bikes without a word. Poppy gave Georgia an apologetic look and went to follow her but stopped when the older girl started speaking.

"Your friend Scarlett won't believe me but I was insanely jealous of her and her brother, growing up on a farm like Ashworthy. I know it was tatty and tumbledown, but I used to love spending time there. It seemed like the perfect life to me."

"And this isn't?" said Poppy, perplexed, thinking of the solariums, the horse walker and the huge indoor arena.

Georgia looked at her feet. "Some things are more important than money."

CHAPTER 8

"That's easy enough to say when you've got millions in the bank," said Scarlett scathingly as they pedalled back to Redhall.

"Sam says they've spent all their money, remember. That's why they had to sell most of Georgia's ponies and take on all the liveries." Poppy swerved to avoid a pothole, almost colliding with Scarlett. "Sorry Red Rum."

But Scarlett wasn't in the mood for make believe any more and they rode the rest of the way in silence. It was only that night as they lay in bed that Poppy decided to tackle the subject again.

"So do you think Angela and Georgia are behind all this?"

Scarlett looked at Poppy as though she was mad. "You bet I do! Look at the evidence. They use Baxters'. They have vacancies. And, most importantly, they have a motive."

"Do they," asked Poppy faintly. It all seemed a bit circumstantial to her.

"Money!" Scarlett declared triumphantly. "Isn't that what everything comes down to in the end?"

A man in a white van pulled into the yard as Poppy was grooming Cloud the next morning. He showed her an identity card on a lanyard around his neck.

"I'm from the water board. I've come to see what the problem is with your supply," he said.

Poppy jogged across to the house and called Sarah, who showed him the stopcock. He scratched his head.

"There's no problem this end. It must be further down the line."

"There's a water leak in one of the fields. I can show you if you like. I was just about to turn Cloud out anyway," said Poppy.

He grabbed a tool kit from the back of his van and followed her to the paddock they'd ridden through the day before. The puddle was even bigger.

"Hmm, this looks serious," he said, pulling out a mobile phone and calling for reinforcements.

Poppy, Scarlett and Sam had finished morning stables and were about to start the weary trudge to the river for water when the engineer reappeared, a satisfied smile on his face. He walked over to the outside tap and turned it on. The three children cheered when a jet of water gushed out.

"Well, I've solved the mystery," he said, showing them two short lengths of blue plastic pipe. "But I can't explain why it happened."

"What do you mean?" asked Poppy.

"Pipes like this are buried about a foot underground and should last for decades," he told them. "But someone had dug down and cut this one clean through."

Poppy, Scarlett and Sam watched in silence as the van disappeared down the Redhall drive.

"I don't understand. Why would anyone want to cut our pipe?" said Sam.

Poppy looked at Scarlett, who nodded and mouthed, "Tell him."

"We think someone's got it in for Redhall, Sam," Poppy said. "That all the stuff that's been happening - the mixed-up order from Baxters', the nuisance calls, the flowers, the water leak - is being done deliberately to sabotage Bella's business."

"That's ludicrous," said Sam. "Why would anyone want to do that?"

"Why do you think?" cried Scarlett. "Use your brain for goodness' sake. They want to steal her liveries."

"But who would want to do that?" he said with a frown.

"Angela Snell and Georgia La-Di-Da Canning, that's who," hissed Scarlett.

"Well, we're not one hundred per cent sure," said Poppy. "But it's certainly looking like it might be."

Sam looked at each of them in turn. Scarlett glared back and Poppy held her hands up helplessly. "We can't think who else it might be," she said.

"I suppose I ought to tell Scott," he said. "Any idea where he is?"

"He's popped into Tavistock. He said he'd be back before lunch," said Scarlett.

"That's another morning stables he's conveniently missed. I don't know why Gran bothered to ask him to come. He's been about as much use as a chocolate teapot."

Poppy silently agreed but Scarlett leapt to his defence. "He did help get the water yesterday. And I'm sure he'll help with evening stables."

"There's a first time for everything," Sam grumbled.

Hoping to head off an argument, Poppy clapped her hands.

"Hey you two, I've had a brilliant idea! Now we don't have to spend an hour fetching water let's take the ponies out for a ride."

That night Poppy lay in bed mulling everything over. Should they phone Bella and tell her what was happening? Poppy didn't think so. Not yet. She had enough on her plate looking after her Auntie Margaret. Should they call the police? Poppy pictured portly Inspector Bill Pearson and his penchant for digestive biscuits. When Poppy and her friend Hope Taylor had turned up at Tavistock Police Station with what must have seemed a dubious account of deceit and duplicity he had listened to everything they had to say - and had believed them. But all Poppy would be able to report this time was a series of events that could be linked but could also be totally unrelated.

Poppy tried to see it through Inspector Pearson's eyes. John the farrier could have misunderstood a call from Bella confirming his visit to shoe Ariel. All it needed was a crackly line and, after all, the phone reception out here was patchy at best. Sarah's theory about someone in the village hearing about Margaret's fall and jumping to the wrong conclusions might be right after all. Perhaps Baxters' had made a genuine mistake and accidentally mixed their order up with someone else's. No matter how hard she tried Poppy couldn't explain away the nuisance calls and the damaged water pipe, but she could see they didn't exactly amount to a vendetta.

And if it was some kind of hate campaign, who was behind it all, anyway? Scarlett was convinced that it was Georgia Canning and her hard-nosed livery yard manager. Poppy wasn't about to rule the pair out either. But they hadn't exactly found any incriminating evidence during their visit to Claydon Manor. And there had been something about Georgia Canning that evening that didn't fit with the win-at-all-costs spoilt little rich girl Poppy had always assumed she was. Although there had been flashes of her trademark snootiness she'd also seemed subdued. If Poppy had been pushed to describe her she'd have said she was lonely.

Poppy checked the time on her phone. Half past twelve. She was physically exhausted yet sleep seemed tantalisingly out of reach. The room was uncomfortably hot. She threw off her covers, padded across the room to the window and pulled open the curtains. The moon was large and low, almost but not quite a full moon. Poppy opened the catches of the Victorian sash window and was just about to heave it open when a movement on the driveway caught her eye.

A hooded figure was creeping along the side of the hedge towards the road. For a moment Poppy was rooted to the spot, paralysed by indecision. The figure stopped and glanced back towards the house. It must have seen her pale face at the window because it turned, crouched down and ran towards a vehicle parked haphazardly on the verge on the other side of the road. The sight of the fleeing intruder galvanised Poppy into action. She tugged at the sash window, but years of neglect had left it stuck fast. Instead she banged on the glass with her fist as hard as she dared. But it was too late. The car was disappearing down the road. Poppy watched with resignation until the tail lights were tiny red pinpricks in the dark and then disappeared altogether.

Her nerves were so taut that when she heard a sound behind her she almost jumped out of her skin.

"Wha's goin' on?" her best friend mumbled. Scarlett sat up and rubbed her eyes. She saw Poppy at the window. "What on earth are you *doing?*"

Poppy started pulling on jeans and a jumper. "I've just seen an intruder. We need to go and check everything's OK. You get dressed and I'll go and wake Sam and Scott. I'll meet you in the kitchen."

Before Scarlett had a chance to answer Poppy legged it out of their room and turned down the hallway towards the bedroom Sam and Scott were sharing. She tapped on the door and let herself in. Sam was asleep in the nearest bed, the frown he'd worn since Scott's arrival softened by sleep. Poppy shook his shoulder. His eyes snapped open.

"What's wrong?"

Poppy told him about the intruder. "We need to check on the horses. I'll wake Scott."

But Scott's bed was empty.

"He's still not back?" Poppy said in exasperation.

Sam shook his head. "I'll text him."

They met in the kitchen. Poppy handed them each a torch and unlocked the back door. They looked at each other, their faces grave.

"I'll check the stables and barn if you two look over the paddocks," said Sam. "Stick together, just in case. And shout if you need me."

Poppy and Scarlett nodded and let themselves out. But when Poppy headed for the yard instead of the fields Scarlett grabbed her arm.

"Where are you going?"

"I have to check on Cloud first, Scar."

She ran across to her pony's stable and slid open the bolt. Training the torch on the straw bed so she didn't blind him with its powerful beam she whispered his name. Cloud opened an eye and whickered. Poppy balanced the torch on the narrow window ledge and threw her arms around his neck in relief.

Scarlett's tousled head appeared over the stable door.

"All OK?"

Poppy nodded.

"Blaze too. Come on, let's go and check on the riding school ponies."

Poppy kissed Cloud's nose and joined her friend. On the other side of the yard they could see the beam of Sam's torch as he looked in each stable.

"How many are out?" Poppy asked. Her brain felt scrambled and she couldn't remember who was stabled and who wasn't.

"Rosie and Buster are in the first paddock," said Scarlett, counting on her fingers. "Salt and Pepper are in the next and Treacle's in the top paddock on his own."

Poppy exhaled with relief when her torch picked out Rosie. The strawberry roan mare was standing in a field shelter with Buster, the chestnut Dartmoor pony Poppy's friend Hope had learnt to ride on.

"We should check them over," said Poppy. The two girls climbed the gate and crossed the field to the shelter. The ponies watched them sleepily as they ran their hands along them and lifted their feet.

"They're fine," said Scarlett. "Let's check on Salt

and Pepper."

The two fleabitten grey New Forest geldings were brothers, bred by Bella out of Rosie's dam, an elderly mare called Conker who was stabled overnight. Salt and Pepper had inherited their dam's easy-going nature and none of Rosie's occasional stroppiness and were the most popular ponies with the more experienced riders at Redhall.

Woken by the sound of voices, the two geldings stood by the gate watching them, their grey ears pricked. Their breath was warm in the chill of the night and they nibbled at the girls' pockets for treats as they were checked over.

"They're OK, too," said Scarlett. She paused. "Are you sure it was a man you saw Poppy?"

"Yes!" Poppy replied hotly, though she was actually beginning to doubt herself. Her eyes couldn't have been playing tricks on her in the moonlight, could they? But no, she had definitely seen the figure and heard the car engine splutter into life.

"Don't get your knickers in a twist, I was only asking," said Scarlett mildly.

"I know it sounds far-fetched. But I definitely saw someone, Scar."

In the distance they heard the rumble of a motorbike.

"Sounds like Scott's back at last," said Poppy. She climbed the gate into Treacle's paddock and shone the torch in front of her, zigzagging the beam to and fro as though she was waving a sparkler on Bonfire night.

"I can't see him, can you?" said Scarlett, who was searching the other side of the paddock.

"Perhaps he's in his field shelter," Poppy said. She directed the torch into the wooden shelter. It was empty. "Perhaps not," she said, half to herself.

"I've checked the rest of the field. He's not here," said Scarlett, her voice rising a level. "Do you think he could have got out?"

Poppy pictured the solid post and rail fences that bordered the Redhall paddocks. Bella was meticulous about maintenance and they were kept in perfect condition. She doubted that even the wayward Treacle could stage an escape. Even so, it was worth checking.

"You check the fences and I'll look behind the shelter. Poppy remembered there was a gap of about a metre between the back wall of the weather-boarded shelter and the fence. Bella used it to store wheelbarrows and the skip and rake for poo-picking. She shone her torch down the gap. The light settled on a perfectly round chestnut rump.

"There you are, you little monkey."

"Any luck?" Scarlett called.

"I've found him!" Poppy shouted. She walked over to him. "Come on little man, let's get you back in the field." She gave him a gentle push. Treacle took a step forward and squealed in pain. "What's wrong?" Poppy cried, shining the torch down. Her blood began pounding in her ears. Rusty barbed wire clung to the pony's back legs like ivy strangling a sapling.

CHAPTER 9

Poppy could see beads of blood where the barbs had pierced Treacle's skin. He tried to free his legs but as he struggled the wire twisted tighter.

"Steady boy," Poppy murmured. "You're making it worse."

Another beam of light appeared around the far end of the shelter. Behind it was Scarlett's familiar silhouette.

"He's caught in barbed wire, Scar. You need to get Sam to call the vet. And see if Bella has any wire cutters. I'll stay with Treacle."

Scarlett shone her torch at the little chestnut gelding's back legs and gasped. "How did it happen?"

"That's not important right now. We need the vet Scar. Just go!"

Scarlett turned on her heels and began running towards the house. Poppy moved carefully up to

Treacle's head and stroked his neck, talking to him quietly. Every now and then the gelding tugged at the wires and Poppy pictured the barbs sinking their rusty teeth even deeper into the thin skin around his cannon bones.

"Hurry up," she whispered into the dark, willing Scarlett to arrive with help. What seemed like hours later she heard voices crossing the field.

"Where is he?" Scott asked urgently. Poppy was sure she could detect a catch in his voice.

"Behind the shelter," panted Scarlett.

Scott appeared with Sam at his shoulder. When he saw Treacle he dropped to his knees and ran his hand along the gelding's back. Poppy could sense Treacle relaxing to his touch.

"Shine your torch on his back legs Poppy," Scott said.

Poppy did as she was told. Scott swore under his breath as he took in the torn skin on Treacle's poor legs. He looked up at Sam, his face ashen. "Pass me the wire cutters. We need to cut the wire before it does any more damage."

Sam handed the solid metal wire cutters to Scott and joined Scarlett and Poppy. He slipped a headcollar onto the gelding. Treacle offered no resistance. His head was low and his normally mischievous eyes were dull with exhaustion. Poppy kept her torch trained on Treacle and they talked in low whispers as Scott snipped away at the barbed wire.

"The vet's on his way. Mum'll bring him straight over the minute he gets here. It's the same one who came out to put Merry down."

Scarlett gave a small cry. Poppy put her arm around her.

"He'll be OK Scar. Though he's going to need a lot of stitches."

"Good job Gran keeps up to date with all their injections," said Sam, looking at the lengths of rusty wire.

Scott stood up and stretched his back. "That's the wire cut," he said.

"Should we walk him back to the yard?" asked Poppy.

"Let's see what the vet says," said Scott.

They all breathed a sigh of relief when they saw the beams of two torches approaching from the direction of the house. Sarah had pulled on some leggings and a fleecy jumper, though she hadn't realised in her haste that she was wearing it back to front. The vet also looked bleary-eyed and his dark auburn hair was dishevelled. But he'd probably been dragged from his bed by the emergency call too, Poppy realised.

"Bella's not having a very good week, is she?" he said, dropping his medicine bag on the floor and stooping to look at Treacle's legs. They watched in silence as he examined the cuts, one by one, under the beam of Poppy's torch.

"He's going to need a few stitches, but it's not as bad as it looks," he said finally, sitting back on his heels. "I'll wash out the wounds with a saline solution and give him a course of antibiotics to prevent an infection. I'll also give him something to ease the pain. But I think he's probably had a lucky escape. If those cuts had been deep enough to damage his joints or tendons it could have been a whole different story."

Poppy felt a wave of relief wash over her.

"Let's get him back to the yard. It'll be easier to do the stitches there." The vet closed his medicine bag and set off with Sarah towards the stables. Scott took Treacle's leadrope from Sam and the gelding hobbled slowly back.

"Let's pick up those bits of barbed wire. The last thing we need is for another of the horses to cut themselves," Poppy said.

They picked up as many pieces as they could see.

"That'll do for now. We'll have another look in the morning," said Sam.

By the time they reached the yard the vet had washed out Treacle's cuts and was stitching the flaps of torn skin back together, a look of deep concentration on his face. After half an hour Treacle's two white socks resembled a jagged patchwork of black stiches. The vet peeled off his pair of blue surgical gloves and ran a hand through his rumpled hair.

"That's him done. He's had a shot of antibiotics and I'll give you some painkillers to add to his feed for the next couple of days. Keep him stabled and I'll pop by in a couple of days' time to see how he's doing."

"We'll put him in Ariel's stable," said Scott, handing Treacle's leadrope to Scarlett. "I'll make it ready for him." He shook the vet's hand. "Thanks for coming so quickly. We really appreciate it."

The vet nodded, climbed into his Land Rover and gave them a brief wave as he drove away into the night. Scott disappeared into the barn, emerging with a bale of straw. He filled the hayrack with a couple of sections of meadow hay and filled two water buckets. Soon Treacle was settled in Ariel's stable, pulling wisps of hay from the rack. Satisfied the pony was comfortable Scott bolted the door and kicked over the bottom door latch.

"Come on, let's go," he said.

Poppy followed the others into the kitchen and accepted a mug of hot chocolate from Sarah with a grateful smile. They sat at the kitchen table cradling the mugs in their hands, deep in their own thoughts.

Sarah broke the silence. "I'll phone Mum in the morning to tell her what's happened." She glanced at the clock above the range cooker. It was a quarter to three. "Well, later this morning," she corrected herself. She drained the rest of her hot chocolate and stood up. "I'm going up. Don't be too late."

They shook their heads. Once they heard Sarah's footsteps on the landing Scott turned to Poppy and said, "Sam told me you saw someone driving away. Tell me what happened."

Poppy described the shadowy figure, dredging up any details she could think of that might help identify their intruder.

"He was wearing a coat with the hood up rather than a hoodie. It was dark grey or black. And he was wearing dark navy jeans," she said.

"He?" asked Scarlett sharply.

Poppy shrugged. "I wouldn't swear on it. But I just got the feeling it was a man by the way he walked."

"And you checked the other horses and the rest of the yard?"

"Everything else was OK," said Sam.

Scott pushed his mug away, as if he suddenly didn't have the appetite for it. "And you think this was deliberate?"

Sam nodded. "Gran hates barbed wire. That's why all the fences are post and rail. You know how careful she is, Scott. I bet there wasn't a single strand of barbed wire in the whole place."

"And yet Treacle was trapped in coils of the stuff. Why would someone want to hurt him? It doesn't make sense."

"They weren't trying to hurt Treacle," said Poppy. "They were targeting Redhall. They want to hurt Bella."

CHAPTER 10

Poppy felt as though she'd been asleep for a nanosecond when the unwelcome buzz of the alarm on her mobile phone dragged her from her dreams. They'd agreed to put morning stables back until half past seven, an hour later than usual, because they'd been so late the night before. Scarlett groaned and pulled her duvet over her head but Poppy climbed stiffly out of bed, picked up her towel and headed for the bathroom.

By the time she'd showered Scarlett had at least got out of bed and was staring out of the window.

"It's too dry for footprints and tyre marks," she said glumly.

"Who are you, Sherlock Holmes?" Poppy teased.

"I wonder what car Angela Snell drives," said Scarlett, ignoring her.

Poppy raised her eyes to the ceiling and headed

downstairs. To her surprise Scott was already at the table, working his way through a mountain of scrambled eggs on toast.

"Scrambled or poached?" said Sarah, waving a wooden spoon at Poppy. She realised she was starving.

"Poached please," she said, pouring a glass of orange juice. "Did you manage to get through to Bella?"

Sarah shook her head. "I couldn't work out why her mobile wasn't working. And then I found this." She pulled a mobile phone charger from a kitchen drawer. "She's only forgotten to take her charger."

"If her phone's dead, how did she phone the farrier?" Poppy pondered.

"Have you tried Great Auntie Margaret's home phone?" asked Sam from the doorway.

"Yes. It just rings and rings and there's no answerphone so I can't leave a message. I suppose Mum's spending each day at the hospital with her. I'll try again tonight."

Scott wiped his last piece of toast around his plate.

"I'll change Treacle's dressings and then give you a hand with the liveries," he said.

He must have caught the look of surprise that flashed across Poppy's face because he added sheepishly, "I know I haven't been much help since I arrived, but that's going to change, I promise."

Scott was as good as his word and once he'd seen to Treacle he began mucking out Cherry and Otto's stables. Poppy had to hand it to him, once he'd made up his mind to help he worked like a demon, finishing both stables before Poppy was even halfway through Paint's. Little beads of perspiration dotted his forehead like raindrops on a car windscreen. He wiped them off with the back of his hand and grinned at Scarlett, who had wandered across the yard with a broom, still looking half asleep.

"Afternoon," he teased. Scarlett yawned and grinned back.

"I just can't wake up," she said. "I reckon we only had about three hours' sleep last night." She glanced over to the drive. "Oh, I wonder who that is."

Poppy pushed the laden wheelbarrow out of Paint's stable and joined her. A red people carrier was crawling up the drive. The sun was glinting off the windscreen making it impossible to see who was driving. The car came to a stop and a slight figure in jeans and a teeshirt flung open the door and jumped out.

"Tia!" cried Scarlett, dropping the broom she was carrying and running over to give her a hug. "It's great to see you, but what are you doing here? There aren't any lessons this week."

"I know. I was going mad at home on my own. I persuaded Mum to give me a lift up," she said. She looked over to the car. Her mum wound down the window, tapped her watch and called out, "I'll see you in an hour."

Tia nodded and turned back to Poppy and Scarlett,

her face suddenly serious. "I just wanted to be with people who were there when it happened. Mum and Dad have been trying to talk to me about it but they don't really understand."

Poppy knew exactly what she meant. No matter how hard she tried not to think about it during the day, at night, when she finally succumbed to sleep, her dreams were filled with images of the accident. Merry somersaulting forwards. Rufus landing on Niamh's back. Scarlett's eyes wide with shock as she screamed. Sometimes Poppy wondered if her dreams would be haunted forever.

Poppy stuck her head over Cherry's stable door. "Is it OK if we finish the stables after lunch, Scott?"

He nodded. "Sure."

"Sam's in the barn," said Scarlett, linking arms with Tia. "Let's go and find him."

Poppy loved Bella's hay barn. From the outside the timber-framed weather-boarded building was nondescript, but inside the feeling of space and timelessness reminded her of a cathedral. Shafts of light danced from floor to ceiling like swirling sprites and although the intense smell of newly-cut hay made her sneeze, Poppy swore it captured the very essence of summer.

As they walked through the big double doors there was a shout - "TIMBEERRR!!" - and a bale of hay bounced down from the top of the stack and landed at their feet. They looked up to see Sam grinning at them from the small space between the tightly-stacked hay and the roof.

Scarlett, who had been playing in hay barns since she could walk, scaled the bales as nimbly as a mountain goat. Tia and Poppy looked at the near vertical wall of hay and then at each other.

"You go first," Tia said.

"Thanks." Poppy stuck a toe between two bales as if she were mounting a horse and pulled herself up. Bale by bale she clambered up the hay, eventually reaching the top. She heaved herself over the last bale and sat down with relief. Seconds later Tia joined her.

Poppy studied Tia's face as she caught her breath. A year older than her and Scarlett, Tia wasn't textbook pretty, but she had thick, wavy dark blonde hair which framed delicate features. Today her eyes were puffy, as if she'd been crying. Which, Poppy imagined, she probably had.

Scarlett was the first to speak. "So, how's Niamh?"

Tia shook her head and bit her bottom lip. "Not good. Mum spoke to her mum last night. She's bruised her spine. She can't move from the waist down."

"Bruised, not broken?" said Poppy, hope flooding through her.

Tia nodded. "At first they thought she might have fractured it but she had another scan yesterday morning and it's just bruised."

"So she'll be able to walk again, once the bruise has healed?" said Scarlett.

"That's the million dollar question, Mum says. She

might, she might not." Tia took a deep breath. "It depends how much damage the swelling has done to her spinal cord and they might not know that for weeks. Even months."

"Poor Niamh," said Sam.

A single tear ran down Tia's cheek. "And it's all my fault."

"No it isn't," cried Poppy.

"Yes it is! If I'd reacted quicker I could have stopped Roof in time. If I'd pulled him left and not right he would have missed Niamh altogether. If I hadn't been there, she would have been fine. Maybe a bit winded, but that's all. Don't you see, I was to blame!"

"You can't think like that, otherwise you'd spend your whole life thinking what if," said Poppy. "Anyway, what if we hadn't cantered? Merry would probably have missed the rabbit hole altogether. What if I'd been riding behind Niamh instead of you? It would have been Cloud's hoof in her back, not Rufus's."

"What if Claydon Manor had never opened a livery yard?" spat Scarlett. "Bella wouldn't have lost any liveries, she wouldn't have had to start holding riding camps, we wouldn't have been her guinea pigs and Merry and Niamh would never have even been on that ride, that's what. I blame Angela Snell."

Tia looked at Scarlett in confusion. "Who's Angela Snell?"

"Doesn't matter," said Sam.

Poppy felt the beginnings of a sneeze fizzing up her nostrils. She pinched the bridge of her nose. "Do you know if Niamh's dad is still planning to sue Bella?"

Tia looked shocked. "I didn't know he was going to. Mum didn't mention that. Anyway, he thinks it's my fault, too."

"What do you mean?" said Sam.

"I wanted to go and see Niamh in hospital to say sorry. Her mum didn't mind but her dad said over his dead body. Mum said she could hear him yelling at Niamh's mum while they were on the phone. She reckons he's probably having some kind of breakdown."

CHAPTER 11

Tia left just before lunch.

"Let us know if you hear any news about Niamh," said Scarlett.

Tia nodded. "And tell Bella to give me a ring once everything is back to normal."

They waved as the red people carrier drove off.

"I don't think it ever will be," said Poppy.

"Will be what?" said Scott, appearing from the barn with a bale of hay in each hand.

"Normal," said Poppy. "I don't think it'll ever be normal again."

Scott dropped the bales, sat down on one and motioned Poppy, Scarlett and Sam to do the same.

"We need to talk about that," he said. "After I mucked out I searched the fields for barbed wire. I checked every fence and hedge. And do you know what?"

"There isn't any," said Sam.

"That's right, Samantha. There isn't any. So how did Treacle end up with barbed wire wrapped around his legs?"

The other three were silent.

"Anyway," said Scott, "it got me thinking about everything else that's been happening since Bella went up to Inverness. And I reckon it's too much of a fluke for it not to be connected." He paused for effect. "I think someone has a vendetta against Redhall."

Poppy exhaled loudly. Sam raised his eyes to the sky. Even Scarlett, for whom Scott could do no wrong, tutted loudly. He looked at them all in turn, confusion in his muddy brown eyes.

"What is it?"

Sam jumped to his feet. "We worked that out ages ago, super sleuth. The question is, what are we going to do about it?"

"We need to put some simple security measures in place. I want to chain and padlock the field gates, make sure the office, tack room and barn are locked at all times - even if we're around - and I want us to take it in turns to check on the horses every couple of hours during the night."

Scarlett groaned. "You're kidding. I'm already shattered! Look at the size of the bags under my eyes! You could do a weekly supermarket shop with them, and I'm not joking."

"Sam and I'll do checks at midnight and two o'clock, and you two can do the four o'clock one.

We're all up at six anyway."

Before Scarlett could reply the phone in Bella's office began ringing.

"I'm not getting it," she said. "It'll be another one of those nuisance calls and they freak me out."

Poppy was about to get up and answer it when Scott jumped to his feet and headed for the office. But before he was halfway across the yard the ringing stopped. Seconds later Sarah appeared with a bag of carrots in one hand and the phone in the other.

"It's a man called Stanley Smith from the Tavistock Herald," she said. "He wants to talk to someone about the riding school, so I suggested he speak to you, Scott." She held out the carrots.

"I don't think that's going to work," he said.

Sarah looked down and laughed. "Sorry. Try the phone."

Scott sat back down on the bale of hay and held the handset close to his ear. Poppy nudged Scarlett, who was grumbling about another broken night's sleep, pointed at Scott and held a finger to her lips. Stanley Smith, nicknamed Sniffer because of his nose for a good story, had once interviewed Poppy and her brother Charlie when they'd seen a big cat on the moor. Sniffer loved a bad news story above all else. Why did he want to speak to someone at Redhall? It didn't bode well.

Scott chewed on a nail as he listened to Sniffer, his expression turning from curiosity to disbelief and then to outrage.

"You've heard *what*? Who on earth told you that? No, it's not true! Yes, the vet was here, but that was to see one of the riding school ponies. No, he hasn't got strangles! He was cut by barbed wire. You need to get your facts straight before you start throwing around accusations like that, mate."

Scott shot up and began pacing across the yard. "What d'you think I mean? Someone's been feeding you a pack of lies. The yard isn't on shut down. We don't have strangles. And if you publish anything to suggest we have I will sue you. And that's not a threat, it's a promise."

Scott ended the call with an angry jab of his index finger and turned to face them. "Someone emailed the Herald this morning to say the yard was on shutdown after two of the ponies were diagnosed with strangles."

He sat down heavily on the hay bale and ran his hands through his hair.

Sarah looked puzzled. "What's strangles?"

"It's a super-contagious disease that affects horses' upper respiratory tracts, Mum," said Sam. "It can cause these really nasty pus-filled abscesses on the sides of their heads and their throats."

Sarah pulled a face. "Not sure I needed quite that much detail, thank you Sam. But none of the horses have strangles, do they?"

Scott shook his head.

"So what's the problem?"

"Don't you see? All it needs is for a rumour to get

out that there's a confirmed case and Redhall's future is on the line. The liveries Bella does have left will be out of here like a shot. People will be worried about coming here for shows. The place will be stigmatised. I know a livery yard that had an actual outbreak. The horses were quarantined and eventually all recovered. But the yard never did. It went out of business shortly after," said Scott.

"Did Sniffer say who told him?" Poppy asked.

"An anonymous email was sent to the newsroom from a Hotmail account."

"No way of tracing it, I suppose," said Sam. "Is there anything we can do?"

Poppy thought hard. They needed to be upfront and quash any rumours before they reached the liveries. "We should phone everyone and tell them what's happened before they hear anything themselves. If they need reassuring they can phone the vet. He'll be able to tell them why he was here last night."

Scott spent the next half an hour on the phone talking to Bella's few remaining liveries.

"How did it go?" asked Scarlett when he finally finished.

"Debbie virtually had a meltdown and was threatening to pull Cherry and Otto from the yard. I did point out that if the rumour was true no other yard would touch her horses with a bargepole until we were clear of strangles anyway. And if it wasn't true there was no reason not to stay. She's going to phone the vet to check, but I think she'll probably stay. Ellie and Paint's owners were both fine. They've kept horses here for years and were more worried about who could be starting the rumour."

"Join the club," said Sam morosely.

Poppy looked around at their worried faces. "Come on, let's go for a ride. Otherwise we'll end up going stir crazy, staying here and worrying about everything."

Scarlett's face brightened. "Can I ride Cherry?"

Scarlett was already sitting on Cherry by the time Poppy led Cloud over to the mounting block. Scott was riding Otto and Sam was on Star. The two Connemaras, one as black as night, the other dappled grey, followed the bay and chestnut thoroughbreds out of the yard.

Scarlett swung around in the saddle. "Let's head over towards Claydon Manor," she called.

"She's obsessed," Poppy muttered to Sam.

"There is a nice ride that goes past the manor house. It takes a couple of hours but we've got time," he said.

"Perfect," said Scarlett. Soon she was chatting to Scott about his job at the showjumping yard. He was a great rider, Poppy had to admit. He sat tall and deeply in the saddle and had the lightest contact on Otto's reins. The big chestnut gelding's long, loping gait was relaxed as he strode out next to his stablemate.

They turned off the road onto the moor and followed a dusty farm track. Cloud felt fresh and full of energy and every so often he snatched at his bit and broke into a jog. Cherry swished her black tail irritably whenever he came too close for comfort. They clattered along the track until they reached a farmyard. Cloud spooked at a rusty plough half buried by brambles and almost collided with Star.

"Sorry," said Poppy. "He's a bit full of himself today."

"There's a great place for a gallop in a minute," said Sam. The track cut through two fields of barley, which shimmered silver green in the sun. Scott looked back.

"Ready?" he asked.

"Yes," said Sam, tightening his reins. Even the perfectly-schooled Star was now jogging sideways up the path. Poppy nodded.

The two thoroughbreds broke into a canter, Cloud and Star hot on their heels. Soon Cherry and Otto were galloping, their hooves thundering like racehorses in the Derby. Cloud lengthened his stride and Poppy crouched low over his neck as he raced to catch up with them. Star matched him stride for stride, their necks outstretched and their manes rippling in the wind. Cloud was strong and surefooted and Poppy felt a bolt of total euphoria that pasted a grin to her face and cancelled out all the worry of the last few days.

The track cut through the barley and climbed the

side of the valley. The four horses galloped up the hill, their tails flying.

"Horse ahead!" called Scott. He pulled Otto back into a canter and the others followed suit. Poppy looked up to see a palomino pony standing as still as a sentry on the brow of the hill. A girl in a candy pink teeshirt with matching silk was watching them intently, a hand to her forehead to shield the sun from her eyes. The four Redhall horses slowed to a walk. The girl spun her pony around and shrieked, "Stay away from us!"

Poppy would have recognised that voice anywhere. "It's Georgia Canning!"

"Why's she screaming at us?" said Scarlett.

Georgia and her pony were now only metres away. "I said stay away! You shouldn't even be out. It's totally irresponsible!"

"What do you mean?" said Scott.

Suddenly Poppy realised. "She thinks we've got strangles!"

Scarlett was shocked. "But how can she? Only the person who emailed the Herald and that reporter know. Unless -"

"-she or Angela were the ones who sent that email," finished Poppy.

Georgia was still screeching at Scott, who was trying to get close enough to tell her that there was no strangles at Redhall.

"I've had enough of this," said Scarlett. She cleared her throat and bellowed, "There's no strangles at

Redhall!" Cherry leapt about three feet into the air. Scarlett didn't bat an eyelid. Poppy wished yet again that she was half as good a rider as her best friend.

Georgia narrowed her eyes and looked Scarlett up and down. "Why should I believe you?"

"Do you really think we'd be mad enough to take the horses out if the yard was on shut down?" Sam said scathingly.

Georgia looked uncertain. Her pony stepped forward and whickered softly to Cloud. She caught Poppy's eye.

"It really is true," said Poppy quietly. "The horses are all fine. But who told you?"

Georgia shrugged. "I can't remember."

Scarlett tutted loudly.

"Please tell us, Georgia. It's really important we find out who's spreading these rumours," Poppy said.

Georgia stared down the valley towards Redhall. Something tugged at Poppy's memory. Something Bella had said about Georgia the day of the affiliated show, when Georgia had beaten Sam to second place.

"Hey, I remember. You used to ride at Redhall, didn't you?"

Georgia glanced at Poppy and gave a faint nod.

"Gran taught you to ride, didn't she Georgia?" said Sam. "Before your family came into all that money. She was always singing your praises. She loved that you were so single-minded and ambitious. In fact she didn't charge your mum for your lessons half the time, did she?"

Poppy saw indecision behind Georgia's eyes and took advantage.

"Redhall's in serious trouble. Someone's trying to put Bella out of business and we need to stop them before it's too late. Who told you about the strangles, Georgia?"

"Angela," said Georgia finally. "She told me while I was tacking up Barley. She sounded -"

"What did she sound?" said Scarlett sharply.

"She sounded *pleased*."

CHAPTER 12

"I knew it!" said Scarlett. "We need to ride straight to Claydon and have it out with her, right now."

"There's no point," said Georgia.

Scarlett's eyes narrowed. "What do you mean?"

"She isn't there. It's her day off. She always drives down to Cornwall to see her parents. She passed me as I rode down the drive. She won't be back until late tonight."

The horses were growing impatient.

"Which way are you going?" Sam asked Georgia.

"Home," she said, pointing to the track in front of them. "Mum helps me do the horses on Angela's day off but she needs me there to tell her what to do."

"Mind if we join you for a bit?" Sam said.

"I suppose not."

Poppy rode Cloud alongside Barley and began telling Georgia about all the things that had happened at Redhall since Bella had left for Inverness. Her china blue eyes widened when she heard about the wire around Treacle's legs.

"I remember Treacle! He bucked me off into a puddle once. Is he OK?"

"He'll be fine, but it could easily have been much worse. That's why we need to find out who's behind all this, so we can stop anything else happening." Poppy paused. "What's she like?"

"Who, Angela?"

Poppy nodded.

"Driven, strict, demanding and really competitive. She's a perfectionist and she hates failure."

"So she would hate it if Claydon's livery yard wasn't a success?"

Georgia nodded. "But there's one thing wrong with your theory. She may play to win, but she loves horses. She would never have hurt Treacle."

"Perhaps she didn't mean to. Perhaps she just left the barbed wire in the field as a warning? Perhaps the wire was already there and what happened to Treacle was a genuine accident and we've just assumed it was part of the vendetta."

"Perhaps," agreed Georgia. "But you won't be able to ask her until the morning."

They rode on in silence until they reached the far boundary of Claydon Manor's huge estate.

"Please don't say anything to Angela. We'll come over in the morning," said Poppy.

Georgia nodded briefly and turned Barley for

home.

"You two seem to have hit it off," said Scarlett. Poppy thought she could detect a touch of resentment in her best friend's voice, though Scarlett had tried to disguise it.

"Not really. I was just pumping her for information," she said. She didn't add that she thought Georgia's haughty exterior was probably shielding a less confident person underneath and that the older girl had looked genuinely shocked when she'd told her about all the things happening at Redhall. If Angela Snell was behind the plot to bring down Bella's yard, Poppy was convinced Georgia Canning knew nothing about it.

The yard was quiet when they finally arrived back an hour later.

"All OK?" Scott asked Sarah as she ladled spoonfuls of tomato soup into bowls and passed them around the kitchen table.

"Not a hint of trouble," she confirmed.

"Well, there wouldn't be, would there?" said Scarlett. "That Snell woman's in Cornwall."

"We'll still padlock the gates and do the checks tonight, just to be on the safe side," said Scott.

As Poppy did afternoon stables she could feel wave after wave of exhaustion sweeping over her. Her eyes felt gritty with tiredness and her limbs were sluggish. She longed to find a quiet corner in the hay barn and sleep for a week. When they sat down to eat Sarah's homemade cottage pie she couldn't stop yawning and after she'd helped Scarlett wash and dry up she announced that she was heading up to bed.

"There's no point me staying to watch TV. I'll only fall asleep. I'll set the alarm on my phone for four o'clock, Scar."

"It doesn't need to take long," said Scott. "Just a quick check on the paddocks and stables to make sure everyone's where they should be and that the gates are locked and then you can go back to bed."

Poppy sank gratefully into bed and pulled the duvet under her chin. She had never felt so bone-tired in her life. She switched off her bedside lamp, curled up in a ball and was just drifting off to sleep when she realised with a start that she'd forgotten to set her alarm. She sat up abruptly, grabbed her phone from the bedside table and stared blearily at the screen.

"Is it even light at four o'clock?" she muttered to herself, tapping the tiny alarm clock icon and scrolling down until she'd reached 0400 hours. She turned the volume up as high as it would go and set the snooze button just in case. Satisfied the alarm was set, she placed her phone back on the bedside table and snuggled back down under the duvet. Seconds later she was asleep.

That night Poppy dreamt she was riding Cloud bareback and without a headcollar across the moonlit moor. She wound her fingers around his mane, gripped with her knees and crouched low as he galloped through valleys and past tors towards Claydon Manor. As they grew close to the boundary of the manor house Poppy saw a huge yew hedge looming in front of her. Cloud lengthened his stride.

"You can't jump it, it's too high!" she cried, tugging his mane, terrified he was going to attempt to hurl himself over. At the last minute she saw a narrow opening the size of a doorway in the wall of yew. Cloud galloped through it without hesitating. They were flanked each side by walls of dark green foliage so high they blocked out the moonlight. Cloud slowed to a trot, and then to a walk. Poppy stared around wildly and shivered as the green walls seemed to close in around her.

In a moment of clarity she realised they were in a giant maze. "We need to head for the centre," Poppy said. She knew it was vital they found the heart of the maze, although she had no idea why.

She used her heels to guide Cloud left and right. They twisted and turned, hitting dead end after dead end. Soon they were completely lost and Poppy could feel panic rising.

Just when she thought she couldn't stand any more Cloud stood stock still, sniffed the air and neighed. An answering whinny echoed around the walls of the maze. Poppy felt a shiver run down her spine. Cloud walked forwards purposefully and she sat quietly, letting him choose his route. Poppy became aware of a pearly glow ahead, like moonlight reflected on water. As they came closer the light became stronger, until it glowed as bright as magnesium. Poppy shielded her eyes. She knew they had almost reached the centre of the maze.

Cloud turned the final corner and whickered. Poppy gasped. Standing in front of them, lit by the ghostly glow, was Merry, with Niamh sat astride her. The bay mare whickered and Cloud stepped forward and blew softly into her nostrils.

Niamh jumped down from Merry and smiled.

"We've been waiting for you, haven't we, Merry?" she said.

Poppy could feel tears welling behind her eyes. "We just kept hitting dead end after dead end."

"But you found us in the end."

Poppy nodded. She slid off Cloud's back and tried to peer around Niamh and Merry. "What's in the centre of the maze?"

Niamh stepped forward, obscuring the source of the light. "The truth," she said simply.

"I need to see it!" cried Poppy. "I need answers!"

"The answers are there, Poppy. You just need to know where to look."

As Poppy leant forward Niamh grabbed her shoulder and started shaking it. "No, Poppy, no!"

"Get off!" Poppy cried. But the shaking wouldn't stop. Poppy felt herself swim back to consciousness. She opened her eyes groggily. Scarlett was standing over her, shaking her shoulder.

"Oh no, Poppy! No! We've slept through the

alarm!"

The image of the dream was still so powerful it took a moment for Poppy to register what Scarlett was saying.

"Wake *up*, Poppy!" Scarlett flung Poppy's jeans and sweatshirt at her. "We need to check on the horses!"

Poppy sat up slowly. Scarlett was already dressed and had pulled the curtains. The bedroom was flooded with light. Poppy checked the time on her phone. Twenty five past six.

"But I don't understand," she gabbled. "I set the alarm last night. I remember doing it."

"You set it for two o'clock this afternoon," said Scarlett, pointing. "Look."

Poppy scanned the screen. Scarlett was right. The alarm was due to go off at 1400 not 0400. She must have accidentally pressed one instead of nought. What an idiot. She grabbed her jeans and pulled them on, trying to ignore the knot of fear tightening in her stomach.

"They'll be OK. It's all padlocked," she said, more to convince herself than Scarlett.

They had reached the bottom of the stairs when Sam bowled in like a tornado. He skidded to a halt on Bella's oak floor when he saw them and looked at Poppy. His face was leached of all colour.

Poppy knew then that something had happened to Cloud. It was her punishment for not setting the alarm properly. She felt light-headed with fear and grabbed hold of the newel post to steady herself.

"What is it? What's happened to him?" she whispered.

Sam shot a desperate look at Scarlett, who put her arm around Poppy's trembling shoulders.

"I'm so sorry, Poppy. He's gone."

CHAPTER 13

Poppy's legs buckled under her and she sat down on the bottom stair with a thump.

"Gone? What do you mean, gone?"

"He was there when we checked at two o'clock. I woke up at six and thought I might as well check on them. Someone had cut through the chain around the gate and it was swinging open."

"Are any of the others missing?" Scarlett asked, her face pale.

Sam shook his head. "Cloud's stable door was the only one that was open. I've spent the last half an hour checking all the fields but I can't find him anywhere. I'm sorry Poppy. He's gone."

"This is all my fault!" Poppy wailed.

"What do you mean?" Sam asked, frowning.

"I set the wrong time on the alarm. We didn't do the four o'clock check. Oh Scarlett, what am I going to do?"

Scarlett sat down beside Poppy. "It's alright. We'll find him, I promise."

"He lived wild on the moor for *five years*, Scar. I couldn't catch him last time. What makes you think this time'll be any different?"

"We don't know he's on the moor," Scarlett reasoned.

Poppy jumped to her feet. "You're right. I need to check the fields again." She marched over to the back door and pulled on her jodhpur boots, Scarlett and Sam trailing behind her.

"Did you check behind the shelter in Treacle's field?" she asked Sam.

He shook his head.

"Well then, that's where we'll start." Poppy set off at a jog towards Treacle's paddock. She scanned the fields for any sign of Cloud, but the only grey ponies in sight were Salt and Pepper, who lifted their heads and watched as she ran past.

Poppy paused at the open gate to Treacle's paddock. Her heart was thudding painfully in her chest. She puffed out her cheeks and blew. Her mouth was so dry it took three attempts before she could muster a half-decent whistle. Poppy held her breath. Normally there would be an answering whinny and Cloud would appear in search of a titbit and a welcome scratch behind his ear. But today all she could hear was the blood pounding in her head.

She raced across the field to the shelter, trying not

to think about poor Treacle's shredded skin. She crossed her fingers and peered around the back wall. But the only thing there was a green wheelbarrow.

She became aware of Scarlett and Sam behind her and spun around.

"I'm going to double-check the other fields too," she panted. She knew she sounded slightly hysterical but she didn't care. If Cloud felt even a fraction of the love for Poppy that she felt for him he wouldn't have run away, would he?

She spent the next half an hour checking and re-checking the paddocks, running to and fro like a kid with a sugar rush. Eventually Sam grabbed her arm and pulled her to a stop.

"He's not here, Poppy," he said.

Poppy knew in her heart that he was right. She looked at him, her face streaked with tears.

"Come on," said Scarlett gently. "Let's go back to the house."

Scott was by the gate inspecting the chain when they tramped back. He beckoned them over.

"Whoever did this must have had a really heavy duty set of bolt croppers," he said, showing them where the metal had been cut cleanly through.

"But why was Cloud's the only stable he opened?" wailed Poppy.

"It's the closest one to the drive. Perhaps he was intending to let all the horses out but got spooked and legged it," said Sam.

Poppy knew he was probably right but it didn't

make it any easier to bear. If only she'd put Cloud in Merry's stable. If only she'd set her alarm properly. If only they hadn't come to Redhall in the first place none of this would have happened. Cloud would be safely tucked up in his stable with Chester, waiting for his breakfast. As it was, he could be miles away, frightened and alone.

Scarlett guessed what she was thinking. "Remember what you told Tia, Poppy. You've got to forget the what ifs. What we need to do is decide what we're going to do next."

"I'll do morning stables so you three can look for Cloud," said Scott.

Poppy ran her hands through her hair. "But where do we start?"

"We'll phone the police and all the local vets and animal sanctuaries," said Sam. "Have you got a photo of Cloud we can send them?"

Poppy thought of her phone, lying on her bedside table. "Hundreds," she said.

"Good. Mum can start phoning around while we go up onto the moor."

One of the things Poppy loved most about Dartmoor was the vastness of it. She loved the sense of freedom and adventure the huge landscapes and sweeping panoramas promised. But this morning, as she trudged down the Redhall drive with Cloud's headcollar on her shoulder and a bucket of pony nuts in her hand, the sheer size of the moor only served to remind her of the enormity of the task ahead. Sometimes, when they hacked out alone on the moor, Cloud would stand stock still, lift his head, sniff the air and Poppy would feel him quivering with excitement. She often wondered if he pined for the freedom he'd once taken for granted. Poppy knew that by bringing him home to Riverdale she'd taken his freedom away and replaced it with a life of captivity and routine, dependence and predictability. What if he hated her for it and longed to be free?

Where would he go? Would he head for Riverdale, pulled by an unconscious force back to the safety of home, the companionship of his stablemate Chester and the promise of a bucketful of breakfast? Or would his flight instinct take over, send him galloping for the horizon, the lure of rediscovered freedom erasing Poppy and Riverdale from his memory?

"We'll check the routes we've ridden on first," said Sam, interrupting Poppy's spiralling thoughts.

She automatically glanced left and right as they reached the road. An image of mangled metal and Cloud's lifeless body pushed its way into her mind's eye like a mirage.

"What if he's been hit by a car?" she cried. Her mum Isobel was killed in a car crash when Poppy was four. Surely fate wouldn't be so cruel?

Scarlett shook her head. "He'll be fine, Poppy. I know he will."

They set off down the rutted track onto the moor, their shoulders hunched and their heads bowed as the track climbed steadily. Soon they were passing the farmhouse where Poppy had called for help. The woman in the red-checked shirt was pegging out a line of washing. She waved when she saw them.

Scarlett waved back. "You haven't seen a grey pony, have you?" she called.

The woman dropped her bag of pegs into the basket of wet washing and walked over.

"A Dartmoor pony?"

"No, he's a dappled grey Connemara, about so high," Scarlett said, holding her hand above her shoulder. "He escaped from Redhall last night."

The woman shook her head. "Sorry, I haven't." She noticed Poppy, who was standing behind Scarlett. "You're the girl who asked to use the phone after the riding accident the other day."

Poppy nodded.

"How is your friend? I've been thinking about her."

"Not good. And her pony had to be put to sleep," said Scarlett.

"I did wonder when I saw the vet's Land Rover. What an awful thing to have happened. And now you've lost a pony, too." She turned to Poppy. "Is it the one you were riding when you came for help?"

"Yes." Poppy swallowed the lump in her throat. "If you see him, please will you phone me?"

"Of course. I'll get a pen and paper and you can write your number down. I'll tell my husband to keep a look out while he's checking on the sheep. And I can pass the word to our neighbours, too, if you like."

"Thank you, that's really kind," Poppy said, smiling feebly.

They asked everyone they passed that morning but no-one had seen Cloud. Poppy's hopes were raised when a couple walking their chocolate Labrador said they'd seen a grey pony drinking from a nearby stream. She raced over, her heart in her mouth, only to find the pony was an iron grey Dartmoor mare with a bay filly foal at foot. She could have wept.

At one o'clock, when there was still no sign of the Connemara, Sam suggested they went back to Redhall.

"We can ride out this afternoon. We'll be able to cover much more ground than we can on foot. We'll head over to Claydon Manor to see if he went that way," he said.

"OK," said Poppy dully, though she knew it was a waste of time. Cloud was gone. And he was never coming back.

Sarah was waiting by the back door and ushered them in.

"I've phoned the three nearest vets, two local animal sanctuaries and the police. There haven't been any accidents and no injured ponies have been brought in. So that's good, isn't it?" she said brightly.

"But no-one's seen him," Poppy said flatly.

The smile slipped from Sarah's face. "No, they haven't. But I've left our number with everyone. He's bound to show up sooner or later."

Poppy's nerves, already stretched to breaking point, suddenly snapped. "Horses aren't like homing pigeons, Sarah. He's not going to suddenly turn up on the doorstep."

Sarah flushed. "I'm sorry. I didn't mean to upset you."

Poppy hadn't thought it possible she could feel any worse. But when she saw the hurt on Sarah's face she knew she was wrong.

"No, I'm sorry. I shouldn't have snapped. It's not your fault. And I do appreciate your help, I really do."

Scarlett banged her forehead with the heel of her hand. "Talk about homing pigeons, you have phoned Caroline to check he hasn't gone home, haven't you?"

Poppy shook her head numbly. In all the panic she had completely forgotten. How stupid. If Cloud was going to go anywhere, surely it would be Riverdale?

Sam passed her the phone and as Poppy dialled she felt a tiny glimmer of hope flare in her heart. Caroline answered on the fourth ring.

"It's me," Poppy gabbled. "Is Cloud with you?"

The glimmer of hope was snuffed out like a candle the second she heard Caroline's sharp intake of breath.

"What do you mean is Cloud here? He's with you, isn't he? What's happened, Poppy?"

Poppy looked at Scarlett, Sam and Sarah's expectant faces and shook her head. She held the phone close to her ear.

"It's a long story."

They set off after lunch, Poppy on Rosie, Scarlett riding Blaze and Sam on Star. Poppy rode ahead, her eyes swivelling left and right as she scanned the horizon for Cloud. Rosie, who was infamous at Redhall for being highly temperamental, had picked up on her mood and she walked meekly as they rode up the dusty track, through the farmyard and into the field of barley.

Poppy's thoughts slipped back to the day Cloud had arrived at Riverdale in Bella's horsebox, his coat matted with blood and his ribs standing out like the wooden bars of a xylophone. She had promised him then that she would always look out for him. And she had broken that promise. It was unforgivable.

The tight ball of fear in Poppy's stomach was morphing into a knot of anger, directed solely at the shadowy figure who'd let her beloved pony out of his stable and in doing so had broken her heart. Life without Cloud didn't bear thinking about. She kicked Rosie into a canter without even telling the others and soon she was crouched over the roan mare's neck as they thundered through the barley.

By the time Scarlett and Sam caught up with her at the top of the hill Poppy had made up her mind.

"I'm going to go and have it out with Angela Snell," she said.

Sam looked at her in consternation. "We don't know she's behind all this."

Scarlett gave him a scathing look. "She has the

motive, the means and the know-how. And anyway, who else could it be?"

"She knew about the strangles," Poppy reminded Sam.

"I know, but -"

But Poppy didn't hear any more. She had already turned Rosie towards Claydon Manor.

Angela Snell was strapping a big chestnut thoroughbred when they clattered into the yard. She greeted them with a steely gaze.

"I hope for all your sakes that Georgia was right when she said there's no strangles at Redhall. Otherwise you'll be hearing from our solicitors."

Poppy jumped off Rosie and marched over to Angela. "Our horses are perfectly healthy. Who told you the yard was on shutdown?"

Angela frowned. "I had an email."

"I need you to show me," Poppy said, handing Rosie's reins to Scarlett. She eyed Angela defiantly, challenging her to refuse. Angela nodded slightly.

"Follow me."

She beckoned Poppy inside the airy office next to the tack room, flipped open an expensive-looking laptop and opened her email account.

"It was sent the day before yesterday," Angela said, pointing to the screen. "There's no name on it."

Poppy read the brief email over her shoulder:

'WARNING: A case of highly-infectious strangles has been diagnosed at Redhall Manor Equestrian Centre. Please

help everyone keep their horses safe and spread the word. Redhall is a no-go area.'

Poppy checked the sender's address. It was a Hotmail account she didn't recognise.

"Probably the same account used to email the Herald." She glared at Angela Snell. "And you didn't bother checking this was true before you started telling people Redhall was on shutdown? What if someone was spreading lies about Claydon Manor? How would you feel?"

"Alright, you've made your point. Anyway, I only mentioned it to Georgia. I've been down in Cornwall with my parents. I didn't get back until nine."

"Nine last night?" Poppy said sharply, thinking of Cloud.

Angela gave her a black look. "No, nine this morning. I decided to stay the night. Why?"

Poppy felt her throat constrict. "Someone let my pony out of his stable at Redhall last night. He escaped onto the moor. We've been looking for him all day."

Angela studied Poppy's face. "That's tough, and I'm very sorry. But if you think I'd stoop so low you are very wrong. Redhall might be in competition with Claydon but I never play dirty. It's not my style."

CHAPTER 14

Poppy lay in bed staring at the ceiling. In the bed beside her Scarlett's breathing grew slow and regular. Once she knew her best friend was definitely asleep she flung back the duvet, pulled on thick socks, jeans and a fleece and slipped out of the room. After less than a week at Redhall she was already familiar with the creaky floorboards and she stepped over them lightly and headed down the stairs, her hand trailing down the polished mahogany banister. In the kitchen she made herself a cup of tea and carried it carefully out into the yard. The moon was full and heavy and it gleamed in the sky like an illustration in a children's storybook. Blaze's chestnut head appeared over her stable door and she whinnied when she saw Poppy.

"Shush, you'll wake the others," Poppy said. She found a couple of pony nuts in the pocket of her jeans and held out her palm. Blaze whickered her thanks and Poppy laid her head against the mare's soft head. "Oh Blaze, do you think he'll be OK?"

Blaze regarded Poppy with limpid eyes. Poppy gave her one last stroke and headed for Cloud's empty stable. She leant on the door, her chin resting on her folded arms. Scott had mucked out while they'd been on the moor. He'd even filled the hayrack and water buckets. She slid the bolt across and tugged the door open. Moonlight flooded into the empty stable. Poppy left the door open wide and sat down in the straw, her hands clasped around her mug of tea. She wondered where Cloud was, what he was doing. Closing her eyes, she pictured his face, as familiar to her as her own. She literally could not bear the thought that she would never see him again.

Perhaps she could try sending him a telepathic message. Poppy didn't believe in that type of thing but surely anything was worth a try?

"Come back to me, Cloud," she whispered, willing her thoughts to span the wide expanse of Dartmoor between her and her beloved Connemara. She sent message after message, pleading with him to hear.

But there was no clatter of hooves on the concrete, no whicker of recognition. She knew she was wasting her time. Cloud had gone and he wasn't coming back.

She thought about their visit to Claydon Manor that afternoon. Poppy felt bad that she'd ever blamed Angela Snell for the vendetta against Redhall. As they'd left Claydon they'd bumped into Georgia, who confirmed that the livery yard manager had arrived home just after nine o'clock. The pair were either telling the truth or they deserved Oscars for their performances. Poppy believed them, anyway. That hadn't stopped Scarlett's lips curling in disbelief when she'd told Scarlett and Sam as they'd ridden home. Scarlett was still convinced of their guilt.

Poppy took a sip of her tea and listened to the sounds of the yard. Horses shifting in their stables, the rustle of straw, the steady breathing of Blaze next door as the mare settled down to sleep. The sounds were soporific and Poppy felt her own eyelids grow heavy. Before long she had nodded off.

Poppy awoke to the oddest sensation that someone was in the stable with her. She froze. What if it was the intruder, come to finish what he'd started? What if he was towering over her right now, his bulk obscuring the shafts of moonlight that had cast a friendly glow over Cloud's stable? Poppy realised her best option was to pretend to still be asleep. At least she would have the element of surprise. She kept her eyes squeezed tight and tried to marshal her groggy thoughts. Stupidly she'd left her phone on her bedside table and the nearest pitchfork was in the barn, which was no use at all. She inched her hand towards the mug in the straw beside her. It was the only thing she had at her disposal. She decided to throw it at the intruder and make a run for it.

Poppy was so focused on her escape plan that at first she didn't notice the draught of warm breath on her cold cheek. She didn't register the feather-like tickle of whiskers against her earlobe. Her fingers curled around the handle of the mug and she drew it close to her chest. And then, in the silence of the stable, a pony whickered softly. Her eyes snapped open.

There, standing in front of her, his face centimetres from her own, was Cloud. Poppy wondered if he was an apparition, an image conjured up by her deep longing for him. She reached out to touch him, half-convinced he would disappear, wraith-like, in a puff of smoke. But the tips of her fingers met warm horse. He stepped forward and gave her the gentlest of nudges. Finally allowing herself to believe he really was there, Poppy jumped to her feet and threw her arms around his neck as tears streamed down her face.

"Oh Cloud, I thought I was never going to see you again. But you came back."

He nibbled the pocket of her fleece and Poppy rested her face against his, delighting in the feel of his soft coat against her skin. She realised she should never have questioned the bond between them. Cloud must love her as much as she loved him.

She gazed into his deep brown eyes. "You could have gone back to Riverdale. But you didn't. You came back to me."

The next morning Poppy and Scarlett free-wheeled into the Baxters' car park and propped their bikes against a green bottle bank. Normally Poppy loved wasting half an hour in the cavernous shop, drinking in the smell of new leather and inspecting the displays of riding gear and equipment, but today her stomach was churning.

"What's the plan? Shall I cause a diversion while you try and slip behind the counter?" whispered Scarlett.

Poppy shrugged helplessly. "I guess. Although I'm not sure what I'm supposed to be looking for."

"All Dad's invoices from Baxters' have his contact phone number on. See if you can log into the computer, open Redhall's account and find Monday's invoice."

Poppy swallowed. "You make it sound easy, Scar. What if I get caught?"

"Look," she said, waving her arm. "The car park's deserted. They only ever have one member of staff on at this time of the afternoon. If it's Tanya we'll be fine. She can talk for England. I'll keep her busy while you do the business. And if anyone sees you behind the counter just pretend you dropped your phone or something."

Poppy frowned. It didn't sound like much of a plan. But, she realised, it was the only one they had.

"Alright, here goes."

She pushed open the double doors and stepped in. Scarlett nodded towards the dark-haired girl sitting behind the counter and gave Poppy a surreptitious thumbs up.

"Tanya!" she cried. "Haven't seen you for ages. How's things?"

"Hi Scarlett. What brings you here?"

"Mum and Dad sent me over to choose a new hat for my birthday. Dad said to stick it on his account."

Poppy raised her eyebrows. Scarlett's birthday was in May, a cool ten months away.

"Sure," said Tanya. "Let me just finish this and I'll come over and measure you up."

Tanya tapped away at the computer keyboard in front of her and, with a couple of clicks of the mouse, the printer chugged into life, spewing out an invoice. She tore it off and opened the middle drawer of a metal filing cabinet behind her. Poppy watched as Tanya's fingers walked along the files until she found the one she was looking for. She pulled the cardboard folder out, slid the invoice inside, replaced the folder and pushed the drawer closed with her backside.

"Right," said Tanya, lifting the hinged counter open. "The hats are over there." She pointed to the far corner of the shop, where a couple of dozen hats were on display on wooden shelving units.

"I'm just going to have a look for a card for Caroline's birthday," said Poppy, edging over to a wire carousel beside the counter.

"Help yourself," smiled Tanya. "So Scarlett, do you want a hat for hacking or are you going to be using it for competitions as well?"

Poppy pretended to scan the arty horse cards and Thelwell cartoons while Tanya and Scarlett disappeared to the back of the shop. After a couple of minutes she glanced up. Tanya was standing with her back to Poppy, holding a tape measure around Scarlett's head. Scarlett caught Poppy watching and winked.

Poppy realised this could be her only chance. She darted behind the counter and stared at the computer screen. It was on the Baxters' home page. Poppy pressed enter and groaned inwardly when she was asked for a password. She tried 1234 and 4321 and then Baxters1234 and Baxters4321, but the computer stubbornly refused her entry. She could hear Tanya murmuring about the new regulations governing riding hats. Poppy abandoned the computer and turned to the filing cabinet. Four drawers, the first marked A-G, the second H-M. Poppy eased open the third, marked N-S, and looked wildly for Redhall. But there was no folder for the riding school. Sure she must have missed it, Poppy checked again. Still nothing.

She thought hard. Maybe the invoices were kept under Bella's name. She slid the third drawer closed and opened the bottom one, marked T-Z. There were five files marked Thompson and Poppy cursed Bella for having such a popular name. Adrenalin coursed through her veins as she pulled out each file and checked inside.

As Poppy pulled out the second to last file she risked a look over her shoulder. Tanya and Scarlett were still deep in conversation, Tanya holding a mirror as Scarlett modelled a skullcap with an emerald green silk. Poppy opened the file.

Bella Thompson
Redhall Manor Equestrian Centre

Bingo.

"So you found the latest invoice?" Scarlett whispered as they pushed their bikes across the car park.

Poppy nodded.

"And there was a mobile number on it?"

Poppy waved her hand in Scarlett's face. "I couldn't find a piece of paper so I wrote it on my hand. It's definitely not Bella's number. I've just checked."

"Don't forget it's there and go and wash your hands," Scarlett cautioned.

"Do I look stupid?" said Poppy hotly. The adrenalin that had helped her through her spying mission was now threatening to bubble into ill temper.

"No need to bite my head off."

"Sorry." Poppy gave her best friend a brief smile. "What did you tell Tanya?"

"That I couldn't make my mind up and that I would come back next time Dad's over. She seemed to buy it. Shall we try the number now?"

Poppy checked her phone. "No signal."

They jumped on their bikes and began pedalling

slowly towards Redhall. At the top of a particularly steep climb Poppy called Scarlett to stop.

"I've got two bars. Shall we give it a go?"

They collapsed on the verge and Scarlett grabbed Poppy's hand.

"I'll read you the number." She screwed up her face. "Is that a seven or a nine?"

Poppy squinted at the smudged biro scrawl on the back of her hand. She'd scribbled it down so quickly it was almost illegible.

"Um, a nine I think."

Poppy dialled as Scarlett read out the number. She felt a flutter of nerves as she waited for the call to connect.

"Put it on speakerphone," Scarlett said urgently. Poppy nodded and pressed the speakerphone icon.

A woman's robotic voice cut through the summer afternoon. *"Your call cannot be completed as dialled. Please check the number and try again."*

Poppy groaned. "I must have written the number down wrong."

"Try a seven instead," Scarlett said.

Poppy re-dialled.

This time the call connected. Time slowed down as the phone rang. Poppy realised she was clutching Scarlett's arm in a vice-like grip. On the fourth ring, just as she was beginning to lose hope, someone picked up.

A gruff voice. "Hello?"

The two girls were silent.

"Who is this?" The voice sounded irritated. "I said, who's calling?"

Poppy panicked. "Er, sorry. Wrong number," she cried, and ended the call.

Back at Redhall they found Sam mucking out Treacle's stable. He listened in silence as they relayed what had happened.

"So we're no nearer to finding out who phoned in that order," Poppy said glumly.

Sam stared into the middle distance. "I've had an idea. It might not work, but it's worth a try. Follow me."

He crossed the yard to Bella's office, tipped Harvey Smith gently off the office chair and booted up the laptop.

"What was the number?" he said.

Poppy checked her call log and read out the eleven digit number. "What are you going to do," she asked.

"Put it into Google and see if it comes up with anything. You never know."

They watched as Sam tapped in the number and pressed search. He hit the top result. A website for a building firm slowly opened.

"Another dead end," sighed Scarlett.

Sam's hand hovered over the mouse, ready to click away from the page.

But Poppy had seen something the other two had missed. She pointed to the bottom right hand corner of the screen.

"Of course," she muttered, replaying the events of the past week in her mind's eye. "It's completely obvious. How can we have been so blind?"

CHAPTER 15

The door to the office swung open and the silhouette of a man appeared. Poppy jumped out of her skin and Scarlett smothered a small scream.

"Three guilty faces if ever I saw some," said Scott, perching on Bella's desk. "What's up?"

"You wouldn't believe us if we told you," said Poppy.

"Try me." Scott yawned widely, showing his chipped tooth. "But you'd better be quick. I was going to sneak forty winks before evening stables."

"Some things never change," said Sam drily. "Poppy and Scarlett went over to Baxters' this afternoon and managed to get the mobile number of the person who made that massive order. And it's him."

Scott studied the computer screen and looked back at them.

"Am I missing something here?"

"It's a building company. Owned by Gordon Cooper," said Scarlett.

Scott shook his head. "Er, still none the wiser."

"Gordon Cooper," said Poppy patiently. "Owner of Cooper Construction."

Scott shrugged.

"Never heard of him."

"He's Niamh's dad."

Scott grabbed his helmet and was threatening to race over to the offices of Cooper Construction to confront Gordon Cooper.

"We know that he made that order, but we can't prove he did anything else, Scott. Not yet, anyway," said Poppy.

"You were sure the intruder you saw was a man, weren't you?" said Scarlett. "Even though I didn't want to believe you at the time."

"And cutting through the water pipe wouldn't be a problem for a builder, would it?" said Sam.

"All circumstantial though, isn't it?" said Poppy. "We need proof."

"But how are we going to get that?" Scarlett asked.

Poppy gave a helpless shrug of her shoulders. "I don't know."

The dinner table was quiet that night, everyone lost in their own thoughts. They'd decided not to tell Sarah about their discovery - not until they had some concrete proof that Gordon Cooper was behind the vendetta. When the phone rang half way through Sarah's mouth-watering apple pie they held their breath as Sarah picked up the phone in the lounge, wondering if it was yet another nuisance call. Poppy felt her shoulders relax when Sarah walked in, a smile on her face.

"That was Mum. Great Auntie Margaret's settled in a nursing home for some respite care until she's back on her feet and Mum's decided to come home. She's setting off shortly and is going to drive through the night. I told her to wait until tomorrow but she insisted. She should be home just after breakfast."

"Did you tell her about all the things that have been happening?" said Sam.

Sarah shook her head. "I decided there was no point worrying her. We'll fill her in when she's back. Anyone for seconds?"

Later, when Sarah had gone to bed, they discussed what to do.

"I vote we do hourly checks tonight. I'll pair up with Scarlett and you two can go together," said Scott.

Scarlett's face flushed with pleasure. "That's a great idea."

But Poppy wasn't going to rely on hourly checks while Gordon Cooper was still at large. "There's no way I'm leaving Cloud tonight, after everything that's happened. I'm sleeping in his stable," she announced.

Sam nodded. "I'm with Poppy on this. I'll bring my duvet down and sleep in Star's stable."

Scott looked at them both in amusement. "You are more than welcome to hunker down with your horses. I, however, need my beauty sleep so I'm afraid I won't be joining you. And if you two are spending the night in the yard you won't need me and Scarlett to do our rounds, will you?" He rubbed his hands together in satisfaction.

Poppy could see the indecision in her best friend's hazel eyes. Scarlett loved her sleep and she idolised Scott but would she risk anything happening to Blaze? Poppy didn't think so.

She was proved right when Scarlett finally stood up and said: "Looks like it's a night in the stable then."

The horses looked on with curiosity as Poppy, Scarlett and Sam dragged their duvets and pillows across the yard and into the three stables. Cloud was the only one who wasn't surprised - at home Poppy often slipped down to his stable in the early hours if she'd been woken by a nightmare and couldn't get back to sleep.

They inspected each other's makeshift beds.

"Looks cosy," said Sam. "So, have you both got torches and your mobile phones?"

"Yes sir!" said Poppy, saluting. Scarlett giggled.

Sam sighed. "I'm just trying to be practical. And we'll text each other if we hear or see anything?"

The girls nodded.

"Is there anything else we should do?" said Poppy.

Scarlett clapped her hands. "I know! We could set

some booby traps."

Sam looked at her as if she was mad, but Poppy's mind was whirring.

"You're right. You know that roll of electric fence wire in the hay barn?" The other two nodded. "Why don't we lay it along the front gate so when he goes to open it he gets an electric shock?"

Scarlett grinned evilly. "Oh yes, I'm loving that idea. And we could arrange those bits of barbed wire he so kindly left on the driveway so he gets a puncture."

"Neat," Poppy said. "What about tying together baler twine to make a trip wire? We could fix it just inside the gate."

Scarlett nodded vigorously. "And I could do the old Tom and Jerry classic and leave a couple of rakes on the ground. With any luck he'll stand on one and whack himself on the head."

Sam's eyebrows were raised as he looked from one girl to the other. "Remind me never to get on the wrong side of you two. You're reprobates."

"He won't be getting anything more than he deserves," said Poppy grimly.

Half an hour later their traps were laid. After Sam had positioned the strands of barbed wire Scott had cut from Treacle's legs across the drive like a police stinger device, he'd wrapped the electric wire tightly around the latch and top bar of the five bar gate and plugged it in. Poppy had tied together a dozen lengths of baler twine and fixed them between two fence posts a few paces into the yard. When she gave the taut orange twine a tug it gave a satisfying twang. Scarlett spent ages arranging and re-arranging the three rusty rakes she'd found languishing in the back of the hay barn.

The last glimmer of dusk was fading into blackness as they inspected their work.

"Good job," said Scarlett, shining her torch at the electrified gate and Poppy's tripwire. "He's going to wish he never picked on Redhall."

"We'd better make sure we get up early enough to take it all down before Gran gets home," said Sam.

Scarlett chuckled. "Good point. We should all set the alarms on our phones for five o'clock."

Poppy yawned, wondering if she would ever enjoy a lie-in again. "Let's try and get some sleep while we can. It could be a long night."

Cloud blew in her hair as she let herself into his stable and she kissed his nose. She wrapped herself in her duvet and wriggled around in the straw until she was comfortable. She closed her eyes and listened to her pony chewing hay. Scarlett was murmuring to Blaze in the stable next door.

"'Night Scar," Poppy called, her voice already drowsy.

"'Night Poppy."

Poppy's limbs grew heavy and her breathing deepened. Soon she was asleep.

Poppy woke with a start and she sat up, looking around her groggily. It was dark. Too dark to see her hand in front of her face. She felt a fizz of fear pulse down her spine. Cloud stirred beside her and she relaxed. He was safe. And then she heard someone tapping gently on the stable wall.

"Scar, is that you?" she whispered.

"I thought I heard a car," Scarlett whispered back. "It's either driven off or stopped, I can't tell which."

Poppy cocked her head and listened. "I can't hear anything."

"Nor can I now. But I'm telling you, I'm sure I heard a car's engine a minute ago."

"I'll text Sam," whispered Poppy, groping in the straw for her mobile. She tapped out a text.

This is a Code Red. I repeat, this is a Code Red. Stand by your stations.

A few seconds later her phone vibrated.

Copy that. I am standing by. Over and out.

Poppy slipped her phone into the back pocket of her jeans, picked up her torch and edged out of the duvet, trying to make as little noise as possible, but every time she moved the rustle of straw seemed to reverberate around the walls. Cloud was staring out of the stable, his nostrils flared as he sniffed the wind. Suddenly he gave a snort and wheeled around, almost knocking Poppy off her feet. She ran her hand along his flank, trying to calm him, even though her own heart was thudding.

"It's OK baby. I won't let him hurt you," she

whispered.

She stiffened as she heard the unmistakable sound of a car door clunking shut. She crept over to the stable door and peered into the yard. But the moon was veiled by thick cloud and she couldn't see a thing.

Was that the crunch of gravel? Poppy strained her ears to hear but it was impossible to tell. She jumped out of her skin when one of the thoroughbreds whinnied loudly, the sound slicing through the still night air like a speedboat through water.

Her phone vibrated in her pocket. She was just reaching for it when a guttural cry and a string of expletives rang out. Scarlett gasped in the stable next door and Poppy's fingers tightened around her torch. She stared into the dark, willing her eyes to distinguish between shadow and shade. As she stared the outline of a hunched figure began to take shape, like a drawing in one of Charlie's dot-to-dot picture books.

It was the same man Poppy had seen the night Treacle was hurt, Poppy would have bet her life on it. And he was heading straight for them.

CHAPTER 16

Poppy narrowed her eyes and watched the hooded figure stumble over the tripwire and curse again. She braced herself for a confrontation as he approached Cloud's stable. But he strode straight past, heading for the padlocked barn. As he walked by Poppy noticed he was carrying a pair of bolt croppers and a red plastic petrol can. It took her a moment to grasp the significance of the can but when she did white-hot anger began bubbling up inside her, giving her courage.

"Oh my God, he's going to burn down the barn!" she cried, sotto voce.

"What do we do?" Scarlett hissed through the wall.

"Call the police. Tell them there's an intruder and they'll send out a patrol car. I need to stop him."

She laid her face against Cloud's cheek as if to draw strength and let herself out of the stable. As she did she saw Star's stable door swing slowly open and Sam appeared, his finger on his lips. He pointed his thumb towards the intruder. Poppy joined him and they crossed the yard in silence. The man had reached the barn doors and had lifted the bolt croppers to the heavy-duty padlock when Sam whispered.

"Ready? On the count of three. One, two, THREE!"

Sam yelled, "Stop right there!" And they simultaneously switched on both their torches. The man dropped the bolt croppers and his hand shot to his forehead as he tried to shield his eyes from the glare of the two torch beams.

"What the -?" he roared, lunging towards Sam.

"Not so fast! The police are on their way," shrieked Poppy, hoping with all her heart that they were.

"You've called the police?" he asked in such a menacing voice that Poppy's blood froze. "Now why would you want to be doing that?"

Poppy watched in horror as he turned his back on them and began unscrewing the top of the plastic can. The noxious smell of petrol filled her nostrils.

"In an ideal world I'd have got inside the barn. But needs must," he muttered to himself, splashing petrol up the huge double doors of the barn.

"What are you doing?" Poppy cried. "You'll destroy everything!"

He turned to Poppy. She kept the torch trained on his face, though the dancing beam gave away her trembling fingers. She lifted her chin and met his gaze. Under a deeply-lined forehead his eyes were emotionless.

"Bella Thompson deserves to lose everything."

He turned back to the barn, reached into his pocket and pulled out a box of matches. "Why don't you children run along and leave me to it?"

Poppy heard Sam move away but her feet were rooted to the ground. She had to keep him talking to stop him setting fire to the barn.

"It wasn't Bella's fault Niamh fell off. I was there. I saw what happened. It was an accident!"

He turned to face her again. "So you know who I am?"

"Gordon Cooper," she whispered. "Niamh's dad."

"My beautiful Niamh is lying in a hospital bed unable to walk because of Bella Thompson," he spat. "She's ruined my daughter's life. And I'm going to make her pay."

Gordon Cooper's mouth stretched into a rictus grin and he pulled a match out of the box, his dead eyes never leaving Poppy's face. He struck the match against the box once, twice. On the third attempt the match splintered in two and he flung it on the floor at his feet. He took out another and struck it viciously.

For a split second the smell of burning sulphur dioxide as the match ignited masked the petrol fumes. And then there was a whoosh as the sleeve of Gordon Cooper's coat caught fire. Poppy screamed as flames darted up his arm and set his coat alight. Within seconds he was engulfed in flames.

Suddenly Sam was at her side, pointing the yard hose at the human fireball in front of them.

"Scarlett, bring one of the duvets!"

Poppy ran to Cloud's stable and grabbed his two buckets of water. As she ran back Scarlett joined her, holding the duvet in her outstretched arms.

"Hold the hose," Sam shouted to Poppy. She took it from him and spurted it at Niamh's dad. Sam took the duvet from Scarlett and threw it over him.

"Now roll on the floor!" he yelled.

Gordon Cooper's dead eyes were now filled with panic. He dropped to the floor and began rolling around on the ground by their feet.

"The police are on their way," Scarlett said, just as the back door slammed and Sarah and Scott came running out.

"What on earth's going on?" Sarah shouted.

Scott took one look at Cooper. The duvet had smothered the flames but he was still writhing around on the concrete, his soot-blackened face twisted in fear.

"Is this him?" Scott asked.

The children nodded.

Scott hauled Cooper to his feet.

"Are you burnt?" he said.

Cooper rubbed his arms gingerly and shook his head. Scott marched him across the yard, flung him in Merry's empty stable and bolted both doors.

"You can stay in there until the police arrive," he said.

The adrenalin that had given Poppy the courage to confront Cooper was seeping away and her legs had turned to jelly. She stumbled over to Cloud's stable, sank to the floor and listened as Sam and Scarlett told Sarah and Scott what had happened.

"Some of the petrol must have splashed back onto him when he was dousing the barn doors," said Sam.

"He's lucky he was wearing such a thick coat," Sarah said.

"And that Sam knew what to do," Scarlett added.

Sam shook his head. "I can't take credit for the booby traps."

"Booby traps?" said Sarah faintly.

"Speaking of which, I'd better switch off the electric fence and move the barbed wire before the police arrive, otherwise they'll be arresting me as well as Niamh's dad." Scarlett headed for the gate, reappearing a few minutes later with a wide grin on her face and lengths of barbed wire, like a deadly bouquet, in her hand.

"Our homemade stinger worked like a dream," she told them with satisfaction. "He had three punctures. Three! He'd never have got away in a million years."

The reassuring sound of sirens grew louder and soon a police patrol car, its blue lights flashing, pulled up behind Gordon Cooper's old van. Poppy hauled herself to her feet and joined the others by the gate. A female police officer emerged from the driver's side, followed shortly by an older male colleague who was talking into his radio. Poppy recognised the female officer immediately. It was PC Claire Bodiam, the kind and capable officer she and her friend Hope Taylor had met at Tavistock Police Station the previous year.

PC Bodiam recognised her, too. "Hello Poppy! What on earth are you doing here?"

"It's a long story," Poppy said.

PC Bodiam took in the petrol can, the abandoned duvet and the strong reek of petrol. "So, who would like to tell me what's been going on?"

She listened in silence as between them Poppy, Scarlett and Sam explained the events of the last week, Scott interjecting every so often.

Soon the two police officers were leading Gordon Cooper away in handcuffs. His head was bowed and he looked utterly defeated, as if all the fight in him had gone. Perhaps he had finally realised Niamh's accident wasn't Bella's fault. Poppy hoped so, for Redhall's sake.

Once he was safely in the car PC Bodiam walked back over.

"He's been arrested on suspicion of criminal damage and attempted arson, although there may well be other offences. We'll know more when we've taken statements from you all," she said. "In the meantime I've just called out our crime scene investigators who'll be here first thing to take photos of the petrol can, matches and bolt croppers, and to examine the barn doors, so please don't touch anything until they've been."

"OK," Sarah nodded. "Thank you."

"No problem," said PC Bodiam. She smiled at Poppy, Scarlett and Sam. "You did exactly the right thing back there. If you hadn't stopped the fire Mr Cooper could easily have died. And Niamh would have lost her dad, just when she needed him most."

"I don't suppose he's going to see it like that," said Sam bitterly. "He hates Gran's guts."

"Oh, I don't know. I think some time down at the station will give him a chance to reflect. I don't think he'll be giving your gran any more trouble. And if he does, you're to let us know immediately," she said.

"What shall we do about his van?" Sarah asked.

"We'll push it out of the way for now and let his wife know she needs to arrange a recovery truck to come and collect it," said PC Bodiam's colleague.

They watched the patrol car accelerate away towards Tavistock. Although the sky was still inky blue a lone blackbird had begun a fluty warble from the hawthorn hedge that bordered the Redhall drive, sounding the first mellow notes of the dawn chorus.

"I can't believe Niamh's dad hates Mum so much that he was prepared to burn down the yard," said Sarah.

"Tia did say she thought he was having some sort of a breakdown," said Sam.

Scott scowled. "That's no excuse for putting the horses' lives in danger."

"I was wrong, wasn't I?" said Scarlett. "I blamed

Georgia Canning and Angela Snell. I thought the motive was money. But it wasn't. Gordon Cooper's motivation was revenge, pure and simple."

CHAPTER 17

Everyone was bleary-eyed but cheerful at breakfast. The nameless threat that had cast its menacing shadow over the riding school for the past week had evaporated the minute Gordon Cooper had been led away in handcuffs. Sun streamed through the kitchen windows as Sarah made pancakes drizzled with maple syrup and freshly-squeezed lemon juice. Poppy wolfed hers down, suddenly ravenously hungry. She was going to miss Sarah's cooking.

They whizzed through morning stables in record time and the horses had all been groomed and turned out by the time the crime scene investigator sent by PC Bodiam arrived in her white van and started dusting for fingerprints.

They showed her the barbed wire and the two pieces of cut water pipe and she photographed the abandoned petrol can, the bolt croppers, the box of matches and the petrol stains on the door of the barn. Poppy carefully undid the dressings on Treacle's legs and held the Welsh pony so she could take pictures of the wounds. The thin skin around Treacle's cannon bones was beginning to heal and there were no signs of an infection but Poppy knew that he would always bear the scars of the barbed wire.

The crime scene investigator was reversing out of the drive when Bella pulled up in her dusty estate car. Poppy ran over and opened the gate so she could park in the yard.

Bella yanked the handbrake up and wound down the window.

"What was a police crime scene investigation van doing here?" she asked, mystified.

"How was the journey?" Poppy asked brightly, hoping to deflect the questions until Sarah arrived. She didn't think Bella was the type to shoot the messenger, but you never knew. She could be a formidable character at times.

Bella heaved herself out of the driver's side and slammed the door so firmly the whole car shuddered. She scanned the yard, her razor-sharp eyes falling on the petrol can. Treacle chose that moment to poke his head over the stable door and give a high-pitched whinny.

"Never mind the journey. Why's Treacle in? Why is there a can of petrol by the barn doors?" She fixed Poppy with a penetrating gaze. "And what was that crime scene investigation van doing here?"

Poppy held up her hands in surrender. "The important thing is, everything is fine now." She lifted Bella's case out of the boot and gave her what she hoped was a beatific smile. "Why don't we go and find Sarah and she can fill you in."

Once Poppy had delivered Bella to the kitchen she wandered over to the paddock Cloud shared with Blaze. She leant on the gate for a while and watched the two ponies grazing side by side. Vaulting the gate, she gave the ponies a Polo each and sat down with her back against the knotty stump of an apple tree and turned her face to the sun. An introvert by nature, Poppy was beginning to crave some time on her own, so she could recharge her batteries. She let her mind drift aimlessly through the events of the past week. She couldn't believe the morning they'd turned up as Bella's pony camp guinea pigs was only seven days ago. It didn't seem possible. This was their last day at Redhall and Bill was due to pick them up at six o'clock. Poppy knew she would be sad to leave after everything that had happened, but she was looking forward to going home. And she and Scarlett still had five whole weeks of the summer holidays left to enjoy. It wasn't so bad.

Scarlett found her in the paddock half an hour later. She waved her mobile phone in Poppy's face.

"Tia's just called. She'd heard about Niamh's dad being arrested and wanted all the gory details. She said it's the talk of their village. But she also had some good news about Niamh. She wiggled her toes this morning." Scarlett collapsed in a heap beside Poppy.

"Does that mean she'll be able to walk again?"

"Not sure, but it's a good sign, isn't it?"

Poppy picked a daisy and began pulling the petals off, one by one. "Pity her dad didn't wait a week before he completely lost it. He might have thought twice about waging war on Bella if he'd known Niamh was on the mend."

"Tia said that according to village gossip his marriage is on the rocks and his building company is about to go bust. There was a fire in his warehouse a couple of weeks ago and the police hauled him in for questioning. Apparently they suspect he started it because he wanted to claim the insurance money. Niamh's mum packed his bags and chucked him out. He's been living in his van ever since. Sounds like Niamh's accident tipped him over the edge."

"That would make sense," Poppy said. "How did Bella take it?"

"I think she's just relieved he's been caught and everyone is alright."

"Is she cross about losing Vile Vivienne?"

Scarlett grinned. "Nope. She said she and Angela Snell deserved each other."

Poppy giggled. "It's a match made in heaven."

The two girls watched their ponies companionably. Poppy twirled the petal-less daisy between her thumb and forefinger.

"We should go for a ride this afternoon. All of us.

And we should go on the Barrow Tor ride. Finish what we started."

"Blimey, that's a bit deep." Scarlett picked a blade of grass and chewed it thoughtfully. "But it's an excellent idea. Let's go and tell the others."

Once again Bella led the way on Floyd. Sam and Scott, on Star and Otto, rode two abreast behind her. Scott was winding Sam up as usual, but they were both laughing - these days Sam gave as good as he got. Poppy and Scarlett rode side-by-side behind them on Cloud and Blaze.

The track onto the moor was bone dry and the horses' hooves sparked little puffs of dust every time they hit the ground. They passed a herd of solemn-faced black and white belted Galloway cattle.

"They always remind me of zebra crossings," Poppy said inconsequentially.

"If you say so," said Scarlett.

Soon they reached the gate to the lane which led past the farmhouse where Poppy had called the ambulance. The farmer's wife must have heard them coming, because an upstairs window was thrown open and she leant out.

"You found him then?" she called.

Poppy ran her hand along Cloud's neck and smiled back.

"Actually, he found me."

They reached the wide grassy ribbon of a track where it had all gone wrong. Bella pulled Floyd up.

"I don't think we'd better canter today," she said.

"I do," said Sam.

"But what about the rabbit hole?"

"It's not there any more. I brought the quad bike up the day after the accident and filled it in."

"Nice work, Samantha," Scott said.

Sam rolled his eyes and tightened his reins. Star tossed her ebony head and crabbed sideways but he sat easily in the saddle.

"So are we going to lay those ghosts to rest or not?" he asked.

"Yep," said Scarlett. Poppy nodded.

"If you're sure," said Bella, kicking Floyd into a canter. Sam and Scott followed suit, still riding side by side. Poppy clicked her tongue but Cloud needed no encouragement. He cantered behind the others, his neck arched proudly and his mane rippling. She crouched low over the saddle as Cloud lengthened his stride and soon they were galloping as one across the moor towards the distant horizon.

Poppy glanced over to Scarlett and was shocked to see a single tear sliding down her best friend's cheek.

"You OK?" she called.

Scarlett nodded. "Just thinking about Niamh."

"Niamh's going to be OK, Scar. I know she is," Poppy said.

And in that moment, as she and her friends galloped across their beloved Dartmoor, the wind in their ears and their horses' hooves thrumming on the springy grass like a beating heart, Poppy knew with absolute certainty that she was right.

ABOUT THE AUTHOR

Amanda Wills was born in Singapore and grew up in the Kent countryside surrounded by a menagerie of animals including four horses, three cats, a dog and numerous sheep, rabbits and chickens.

She worked as a journalist for more than 20 years and is now a police press officer.

Four years ago Amanda combined her love of writing with her passion for horses and began writing pony fiction. Her first novel, The Lost Pony of Riverdale, was published in 2013. The sequel, Against all Hope, followed in the summer of 2014 and Into the Storm was published in January 2015. Redhall Riders is the fourth book in the series.

Find out more at www.amandawills.co.uk or like Amanda Wills Author on Facebook.

Printed in Great Britain
by Amazon